love and the fear of love
(which is also love)

For Mom

Copyright © 2023 Norman Douglas

Published Exclusively and Globally by Far West Press

All rights reserved. No part of this book may be reproduced in
any form or by any electronic or mechanical means, including
information storage and retrieval systems, without written
permission from the publisher or author, except in the case of
a reviewer, who may quote brief passages in a review. Scanning,
uploading, and electronic distribution of this book or the
facilitation of such without the permission of the publisher is
prohibited. Your support of the author's rights is appreciated.

This is a work of fiction. All names, characters, businesses,
places, events, and incidents are either the products of the
author's imagination or used in a fictitious manner. Any
resemblance to actual persons, living or dead, or actual events is
purely coincidental.

Cover and Back Cover Illustrations: Public domain images.
Taken from "Songs for Little People. [with illustrations by H.
Stratton.]" Author: Gale, Norman Rowland. Contributor:
Stratton, Helen. Original Publication: Constable & Co.
(London) 1896

www.farwestpress.com

First Edition

ISBN 979-8-9858067-6-2

Printed in the United States of America

Contents

JUDGE: let the record show that defendant is indicted on the charge of fear of love and has entered a plea of innocent. prosecution proceed.

DISTRICT ATTORNEY: what's your relationship to the dead?

PERP: it ain't my bizness.

DISTRICT ATTORNEY: who says?

PERP: they did.

DISTRICT ATTORNEY: how did that happen?

PERP: i called and they said, "i'm dead, so nunya beeswax." i said "i got a coffin." i thought i could help.

DISTRICT ATTORNEY: wtf?! your honor, let the record show that perp thought he could help!

PUBLIC DEFENDER: objection! just bc he thought he could help doesn't mean he actually helped!

JUDGE: no one can help; and the thought shows a superiority complex, pre-meditation, plus prejudice. overruled. proceed.

DISTRICT ATTORNEY: so, you help people. how much do you charge?

PERP: well, i mean, i love em. i never ask a lot tho, tbh. just communication.

DISTRICT ATTORNEY: you? honest? not a lot? so a little's like: you text, they text you back? you question, they answer?

PERP: i mean, if they can say they dead, then they

can say anything. somethin. i know it don't mean nothin. but the silence. ugh.

DISTRICT ATTORNEY: tsk, tsk. so much disappointment. poor thing. as for silence, you should be grateful for the peace. but you say "i love you" and want "i love you" back. right?

PERP: i love you more.

DISTRICT ATTORNEY: bwahahaaaaa!!! you got jokes? ok... so they're dead. then what?

PERP: they move in, they move out, they want nuthin, they want kids, they cash in the special romance coupon at the new bae shop and stop. to me, i mean. ghost. i'm embarrassed to say anything.

DISTRICT ATTORNEY: so, you're terrified of love. and you wanna shift the blame. even when there's no blame.

PUBLIC DEFENDER: objection! embarrassment is guilt not blame.

DISTRICT ATTORNEY: guilt is self-blame. it's contagion. it's fake humble and grandiose ego-love of fear.

PUBLIC DEFENDER: but that's also wholly love and allowed!!

PERP: i just wanna be alone like before! lonely sucks! i miss all-one alone!

JUDGE: omg quiet! *before*? i heard enough. boy, you's afraid of love. i hereby sentence you to love. love: it ain't you or a thing or people. you can't hit it and quit it. no attachment detachment surfeit deficit order. you can't see love. love is love. the rest is special illusion toy illusions to play with. love don't care. try light or e=mc squared. ya square! dismissed!

no one questioned why the dusty book-n-brewhole still operated on the ever-changing promenade. the last next generation ventured inside looking for "interesting" and "old" and were surprised to find the owner was barely thirty. she couldn't possibly know as much about books as the mainly graying clients, few of whom recalled when *they'd* last held a book!

tall and sturdy, clarice chatted flippantly with her trickster jaw to patrons who stayed for a beer upon learning the old taps dispensed local brews with quaint names.

the day andrea turned up, clarice felt an ancient mojo zero in on her vital youth ciphers. "hold on, everybody!" shouted clarice and rushed to the bathroom. relieved when close study of her mirror image proved andrea's hairy gray eyeball was all-show-not-shaman, clarice returned to the shop floor.

andrea gripped her arm and clarice went limp as a kitten scragged at its scruff.

"andrea?" stuttered clarice, astonished to utter the name.

"i'll wait til you close," andrea croaked, shrewd, emphatic.

on their way to her flat, clarice told her story. "the owners left it all to me when they died. they told me you'd lived here. but not about willy. they musta thought i'd be scared. at first, i was. but i guess ya can get used to anything."

"he touched you?" andrea spat, pissy.

"he talked about you: you said he was special, then left for a better guy so willy died," clarice recounted.

"i left that better guy for a better guy," scoffed andrea.

"i bet willy knows you're here."

"he fukn better! he fukn touched you!"

"uhh, i don't think it's healthy for ya to get all riled up."

"eat it, ya lil bitch! when i was yer age, i'da bashed yer stupid face!"

when she saw willy seated blond in the kitchen tinkering a thing, andrea said, "hey, bud!" she choked on tears. "you haven't aged a day! you're special af! but why ya still got that rope round your neck?"

"what rope?" said willy. "i ain't here."

"stop!" yelled andrea. "kiss me!! you kissed this bitch!"

"but i ain't here."

"i love you!" keened andrea.

"i ain't here," he said.

andrea's heart attacked her.

when clarice finished 911-ing, she sat on willy's lap and said, "she ghost." "

"me too, boo!" woowoo'd willy.

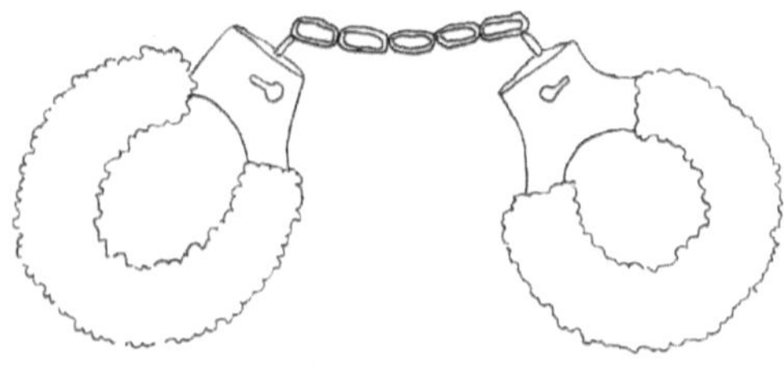

one beltane eve, maleagant sent a phynnodderee — naked and hairy as the day he was born many thousands of years ago — to kidnap lil queenie. he tore her from the communal beds of seagrass carpeting the sandy shallows where scallops repose by a causeway connecting meliagrant's ugly norman castle to the lush island off of avalon. until the day luanistyn keeps night sky at bay, queenie suffered meliaganz' wicked ravishings with bravery and a faith largely due to cants and verses the remorseful fenodyree trilled whenever the despoiler retreated to hell knows where.

when, at last, king and knights confirmed meleagan's crime and lair, the fenodderee and moddey dhoo the ghost dog led them to the diabolical dungeon. meliagaunt was bound and put to the ling chi — death by a thousand cuts. moddey dhoo refused the chunks of fetid flesh, and the sea turned green when the madman's minced meat was finally cast into the waters on the third day.

thanks to queenie's testimony before the weird court of scallops and men looking into details of her abduction, the phynodderree was deemed innocent of crime, for mad mellyagraunce had forced the imp to wear clothing, an abomination no fynnodderee can endure; like a poison rat tears headlong for open air — yet without mercy of immanent death.

for the salve his songs lent the once captive lady of the half-shell, king art declared he would gift the two-foot tall but magisterial and heroic phenodderee any reward he pleased. the dear fey one wept for glee and grace, blubbering briny tears amid his wish "only to be seen as big brother of the lil queenie." and since merlin was there as judge, it was so. and they danced.

meanwhile, pissed off by toxic mellegrans' meat slivers greening the sea, a glashtyn — amphibious, with a bull's head and a horse's body — arose from the waves and galloped through the gathering, snatching lil queenie away to live with him in wild wandering abandon under the seven seas. however, the glashan endorsed the siblings just as merlin decreed, returning to court on the eight solar feasts so that everyone enjoys all the phynnodderee's serenades to lil seastar queenie at the sand bars.

and so it is to this day.

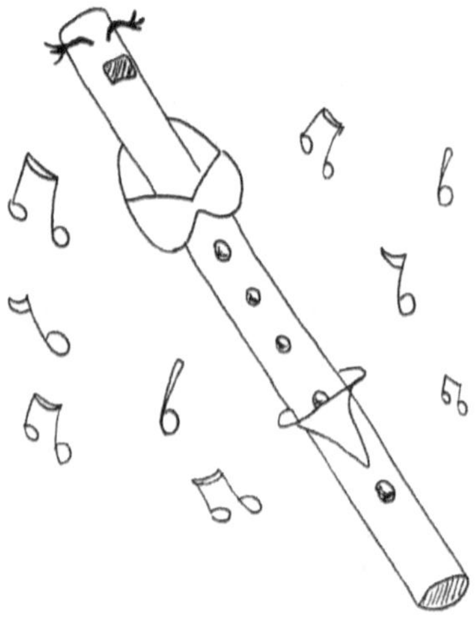

lester's compatriots believed he'd gone native, taking pri with him. what baffled them was his theft of twelve trousers.

in fact, lester vowed to god and pri that he'd get a dozen tantric zealots to wear slacks for civilization's sake. he gave crimson britches to pri to usurp her bright sari. she didn't care. his was a losing battle; it was lester and his ilk who lacked refinement, which was kinda cute to pri. she giggled at his clueless dismissal of what he deemed her dizziness.

the day an ancient yogi donned the last purloined pants, lester and pri scurried into the bush to shed their knickers and fuk.

macaque mike spied pri's crimson rompers. he snatched them, tore a hole in the seat seam for his tail, put em on, and scampered up a tree.

lafcadio the tiger spotted mike and asked, "what the heck's on your legs?"

"that guy fukn there told her that 'the trousers will be safe here.' then they shucked em off to get busy! now I'M safe here!" he pointed at lester's navy slacks. "LOOK! he left you one!"

"well i'll be a monkey's uncle," said lafcadio.

"how do i look?" asked mike.

"like ya got no balls and dick," growled lafcadio. after a moment of purring raptly, he clawed a hole for his tail and slipped into lasters's breeches. "look at me!" he roared. "i'm scum o de earth!"

"they fit you perfect!" snickered mike.

the roaring startled our fuckers, who stopped to listen.

"my bloody pants!" yelled lester. he peeped lafcadio. "oi! those are mines, pal."

lafcadio snarled fiercely, "i'm bossypants now, bro!!"

"pundit!" pri piped in, "pussy and dick hide in trousers so boy and girl learn fucking is secret and special even tho it's sacred nature portals thru eternity for none and all. pants curse root!"

"i got big balls!" yelled lafcadio.

"i got tiny nuts but a big fam!" mike tittered.

leona lioness appeared, reeking oestrum. "stick sumthin in me," she mewled in all directions, rubbing scut on a mandrake.

"i guess it's my job!" screeched the mandragola, naked from branch to the rhizome he was born of. "i'ma drip ya a little sperm spilt by the hanged man who sired me!"

and so, the naked root rutted the big puss til she yowled uncle and vomited up three squiggling little furball cubs.

the instant the eyes open, they close. the ears have a chance to give a listen around, the hiss of the embers, the quiet through the windows occasionally punctuated by the soughing of tires on wet asphalt beyond trees that surround the meadow by the water where the peepers grow quieter in the graying of the morning at night's end. a listening that puts aside a thought of going to buy groceries and pushes down the phony need to consider calling mom and sighs to forget about seeing a friend who isn't here when the bed is soft enough and warm enough and close enough to every inch of the skin to simply lay there with the shoulder blades cushioned like wings captured by a neighborly wind that carries nothing too far or fast, toes wriggling at the bedclothes' undersides as prelude to stretching one limb before a next just far enough to draw them back into a curl that leans onto one side for a breath rushing effortlessly deeper than a sigh and drifts the dream of life almost awakened off for a further bout of soporific bliss.

and now the sun is high and so is the moon, but there's no one who asks the planets for whereabouts when the air keeps hanging around without a detailed plan to stave off a hunger that will come if this doesn't feel so easy to chill later when time starts ticking off impulses to try what a little patience nullifies left to its own devices without interference from morphologies of angst and desire returned to dismiss the boundless energy a want reflects. no one is telling stories of tales that can't be told by chaos birdsongs' unsung melodious chorals to scores no less or greater than this overhearing freed of looking to make a giant step outside or in or over.

and now the grass is a carpet and the clothes are
ragged and loose and the streaks that dart across the
bright blue day that shuts the eyelids overfulfilled
with light playing at dragonfly or hummingbird
or buzzing bee and bluefly tuned in to the cicadan
harmonies entwined thru toad and grasshopper
gripping the bow-springing fronds rippled ripshod
over gold in fields of haw.

all this because ...

-- text breaks off here {ed.]

it was only cloudy an hour after it was not.

she loved her motorcycle: the sound of it, the size of it versus cars and trucks that shared the road, how the road kept coming up to meet it as long as she kept it going. but lately, it didn't help her forget her balls. she lost them and couldn't remember where. she suspected it was all her fault and made it her story. she didn't wanna call the cops. she didn't trust cops. cops depend on snitches, and snitches lie. it was a road that didn't end ok, if at all. to this end, she went to bars. she stopped in at mars and knocked back a whisky. she rode to siberia and chugged a beer. at lakeside, she downed some mezcal. inside lupo's, she sipped red wine. bellied up in the kraken, she finished a gin.

the weather was perfect and she stepped out for a cigarette. when she perched a butt between her lips, a dark-haired woman already smoking there reached out to offer a light. "drinking?" she said as the tobacco sizzled and glowed and released a swirl of white fumes around their faces.

"and riding," the rider smiled.

the lighter grinned. "my buddies run a cheap speak and flop at their crib. come over."

"when?"

"right now."

"where?"

"follow me."

"you didn't say 'simon says.'"

"i only play serious games."

it was a big addams family house, with six scary

monsters on the porch arguing about the reasons they hated the potus, forgetting their hates were an agreement, as was their resolve to argue hatreds.

"who's this?" snarled a dwarf with the flat snout and caved-in mug of a pugilist.

"she's drinking," said the dark-haired woman.

the chthonic fighter sniffed hard and deep as if the smack in his nose was running out.

"what's she drinking?" barked a burly lady whose snake tattoo started with its tail on the tip of her nose as the rest of it curled into a sideways eight all across her wide brow.

the rider said, "vodka this time."

"it's on me," said the woman she followed. inside, she kissed the barmaid who handed her a bottle of stoli she then poured down her face and neck and breast and belly and hips and thighs. "it's on me!"

the bike rider set about licking and sucking. maybe this is how to get my balls back, she thought in a haze of quiet excitation.

it was a small wooden structure past the end of a quiet town's single road that sloped to a ford. there was no sign on the door but a single branch of haw hung by a rusty nail spoke to him, and he knocked. the rain cascaded from the black sky and the swollen river lapped at the cabin's stone feet.

a woman of monstrous beauty gently opened the door inward and smiled at him with an icy warmth that mirrored the glassy pools of darkness beamed through the spectrum of color that shone in the maelstrom of her eyes. "you poor old fool. you're soaked. come on." she gestured and turned and bent her back to open the wood stove, heaved a log from the small pile into the fire. she sat at the worn table on a low, three-legged stool. "sit."

he felt his body warm and saw his clothes drying on a line. he was naked. "you can't drown in love," she told him. "we're fish. and love is the ocean. but you don't know or believe that. you're a sailor with no shipmates. you can't remember why they're gone because you left them. and all for some mermaid. you poor old fool."

he sat transfixed, unsure that he saw her head rise from barely above the tabletop until her whole figure — still seated — seemed bigger than him; so that the room he felt dwarfed him also closed in on her. she was a child, then a hag, a young mother, then him. and the mermaid. her fingers fiddled with the heap of dried leaves and twigs that covered the worn butcher block surface with the fragrance of fecund earth and its microbial mycologies recomposing invisible phosphors and alchemistries of wood and green sweetness. "i can't stop you drowning because you're

not drowning. i can't return love to you bc you can't
lose love. a fool's thoughts believe energies transmute
into a dramatic weakness mistaken as a desire for a
beauty already achieved as imagined. you can't dream
of what is not. you fear love. i am dumb to you. mute.
these thirty three medicines are mixed to cut the
power of the herb you think you want. if you drink
the tea in the pot on the stove, no one knows when or
what blowback i'll suffer. but first, i will ferry you as if
for the island. your mermaid will come. you will dive
in without hesitation."

dead at last, i packed the hoopty, headed south. uniforms waited at the river, weapons ready. a short one strolled by the passenger side, peered in. a big dark burly no-neck in wide eyes stood on my side, looked at me like i knew what to do. it knocked on the door. i opened it up. i got out and stood before it.

"what the hell you doin?" it asked.

"i dunno. ya knocked on my door so i got out. ya want me to get back in?"

"freeze!" hollered the other one, running my way all crazy legs, heavy and loud. i didn't move.

a salamander skittered just out of sight to the water. a crane soared high, followed fluxes. chipmunks yelled at us from a giant woodpile. i heard fish jump after dragonflies hunting skeeters.

"get back in the ride!" hooted no-neck.

"wtf? that guy says freeze. you say get in. if neither of ya's wanna be in charge, i'll take over."

"get some ID!" shorty shouted at the big. "they got animals!!"

"what's goin' on? it's hot as hell! we're late!" the chimp riding shotgun piped in.

"turn the car on," i said "if ya really wanna fuk up the ozone some more."

"that monkey talked!" said no-neck.

"what are you a scientist?" wondered the black cat seated on the seatback.

"i *told* you they got animals!"

"SARGE!" howled no-neck. "we need metrics."

"nobody move," ordered shorty, weapon pointed square at me.

sarge appeared twirling his mustache next to a woman in a tight pink dress and heels carrying a black plastic box with wires. "come here, you!" sarge snarled.

"yessir, sarge!" i obeyed. no-neck and shorty marched on either side. a committee of vultures steadily grew in number atop the official architecture.

"if you hurt daddy, we'll bite and scratch ya's all silly," howled the redcoat lab in the back of my ride.

"wtf was that?" sarge squealed.

"he has animals!" shorty ratted on me to its boss.

"they talk!" added no-neck.

"plug him in!" sarge ordered the woman.

"only if i get to plug back when your foolish metrics fail," i warned.

she plugged. i felt a pinch. the whole kaboodle sizzled, sparkled, backfired loud af, then blew the uniforms sky high. the sweet pink lady aka the silent boatman bit into my flesh and invited the menagerie and me to sing and dance on their yacht.

they didn't see the eagle lift itself up from its nest, nor its nest. but they both pointed as one when it soared low between the sun-drenched trees that stood watch beside the wide and shallow creek echoing with secrets of drift and swerve both water and wood mirror in each other; not unlike the imperceptibly moving stillness of stone and sky conform to earth's enduring fundament as the heavens' unfathomable firmament.

"was that a coincidence?" the old woman asked the younger. "or do you have the sight our dead rarely whispered?"

the young one laughed. "i can't honestly say i can see what can be seen now by me, never mind the two of us."

"but you're content."

"you can't see what you're not. and you're not a liar."

and then, listening.

"i was scared when i was young. i'm scared now."

"scared of what? listen. there's nothing."

"death is far from you, tho. my time is near its end."

"so it is." the young woman let her hand rise from the coarse rock that held their perinea until her fingers found the old woman's back. "and when time comes to its end, death and life are cleared away with memory, and you'll be nothing, eternal without knowing how. kinda like now."

the old woman sighed. "i never had a plan. i traveled among travelers and roomed with those who stayed close to home. i enjoyed great beauties and suffered deep pains and wondered why there was so much — none of it enough to call it mine."

without releasing her pressed hand from the electric push of the old woman's slumped shoulders, the young woman nodded at a smooth black river rock that lay heaping itself toward the leap and swerve of the watery onslaught the sunlight played upon so that the clamor of spills splashed and joined to engage the seemingly inexhaustible energies of a dance she called: "an eddy among a flow that feels endless. i can't share the dream that separates us. there's no difference without sameness, and we're not the same. let the unreality of unseen space between us collapse so that we are not here to go nowhere. because everywhere. can this peace dreamed be without a purpose that sorority caused for an effect? identity in dreams is meaningless; in dreams, dreamer and dream are one."

there were other guys acting like they cared about her: the dj, the shrink, the artist, the poet, the drunk, the doper, the wifebeater, fools. but he played number one, believed she wanted help; to feel better, to replace destructive behaviors carried from a past lousy with abuse pushed to extremes. he said he could steward her through that morass into a vulnerability of deepwelled, abiding trust.

of course, his confidence wasn't the integrity of a shamanic tribe's intonal cycles uttering unitary and communal sanctification of the everyday — an iron god whose rust manifests on a par not exclusive to polish, a water goddess whose nectars reveal snowflakes and sap without preference over sweat, blood, tears, piss — speeching to unlearn nothing of the valorous attainment of transcendent knowledge as furthered individual purpose (however benign a fake self holds its quiet intent to reap humble rewards of selflessness). his was a heroic mission that would stop her imitating punching bags, emotionally torn and spilled empty paper bags, used scumbags. he didn't offer any other bags but saw that she enjoyed retreating to shopping bags abounding with thrifty booty, found things, chance discoveries that drew a keen eye for simple treasures resplendent with beauty. he didn't encourage this, but welcomed the signs of pleasures and joys her terrors would never snuff out.

he saw her pouring buckets of hope at the sunrise of a tomorrow promising a river of forgetfulness that never comes from or goes anywhere, not even here or now. he felt pleased without being moved by this hope, certain that his ideas of love delivered levities free of judgment, yet eminently enlightened.

and then, she was dead.

he wasn't sure if it was she or he or one or all of the fools that killed her or maybe she simply dropped dead as all betray how the naked must hide in life. he soon doubted the role he'd assumed as if long dark knight of the soul in tarnished armor could ever provide a satisfactory percentage tantamount to his investment or hers, the memorized lines, the shifty response abilities, the quixotic, the unlimited unnecessaries of unconditional love or whatever it's called.

who could blame us?

no one, of course. only one fear leads to an impasse at the tail end of an enclosure she allows to confine her with all she needs to compartmentalize fragments of feelings that needle and poke with persuasive persistence. for she imagines the soup of confusion harasses her with thoughts of escape into the constancy of wild and cyclical nature's ungovernable reliability.

he is no different. his jumbles of meanings pretend to order a chaos that delivers silence as the menace underpinning each chimerically consecrated conversation his deftly invisible friends attempt to denigrate as counterbalance for the grandiosity of his humble exterior and the surroundings they favor.

and around them, the headlines and broadcasts of words they quietly ignore embolden whole populations to bully an unholy populace into hiding, astounded by the defiance of those who go home later, earlier, and around the same time, no matter what they sound like between the thin masks of a mass comportment.

who dares to face down the fear of love? the death it demands of a body promises nothing but surrender to the patience of a permission that needs no thing more necessary than it already is and must be.

she breathes with air that gives what it takes, like the trees and oceans embedded in an earth that swallows everything it lets go through the blackness of a planet encrusted as if twinkling light into an empty and timeless absence of property, walls, portals.

a kiss: not for his lips, not for hers, remembered where memory lapses in its wild gesturing for controls ineffectually devised for what this is and never becomes.

terrorized by never wanting to dance alone, this choreographs not what i write or what's right, its rites performed without script or stint that replay an unspeakable peace uncollected into a report repeated so perfect as psyche wedded to love like no secret bedroom witness soars through this wide unified open sky, unbroken like flickering bonfires spitting sparks fat manatees spout as sirens gone naked while a whale bellies up the eye of a pinewood boy drifting the seas.

or who is never truly afraid of seeing the fear of why love won't leave us alone?

moon water collects on grasses in darkness to steady retreat into soil. bodies huddle close near a rivering. sky fire rises. invisible flame spreads inside the air.

deep dreamtouch stirs this body unwinding between maisy and sosa. sosa moans softly fucking banto. maisy arouses us with a gift, a rub, a waking excitedly joined.

slowly, smashing of flesh releases cool night from muscle and organ. stretching bodies push wild polyrhythms pulsed ever closer to common sameness. throbbing delights burst forth as loin spasms sharing bright laughter.

then, most of us piss. some shit. the babes suckle, nursing.

small bodies run, screeching round the waning fuckcircle of dreamtouch.

woodpeckers point at food in trees. our limbs climb us up to find holes they made. larvae are fat sweets munched as we drop many for brothers and sisters scooping savory fare and humming...

insects creep and buzz. wintering cave sleeps alone a moon cycle's walk behind us. trees grow great girth and height slow, unseen. long reaching branches drip wet under feet.

maisy and sabu smell salt calling the rivering. we follow the chattery sploosh and clear sparkle. widening and deepening happen where swoosh meets thinner flows. we carve paths downhill to easy terrain. thickening underbrush greens this lush forest cover.

bellies compel bugs and mykos to refill what shitting emptied. foraging in twos and threes reveals abundance under the canopy. we mimic bird signal

and animal speech, track droppings and greenings,
find meats, eggs, fungus.

sky fire passes its high perch. we stop to share
skinning and gutting of squirrel, cock, pigeon, fox
attained through stealth and speed.

after thirteen great moon cycles, sisters and
brothers are quick hunters. in wakefulness they lead
the catching. they hold and push their slim bodies
close. they join happiness singing with all.

day nurses unsling swaddles. mothers climb out
the rivering with turtle and frog and fish aplenty.

and so this is this.

and on, watching black sky and blue sky fires
enliven songwalking lands unto the great salt water.

they rushed into it. he found her honey colored face and wide mouth magnetic. her dulcet voice sang through the dark behind a glistening moistness grown around tight little bubbles of spit that leapt between the plush mounds of her purple lips and the oily mother of pearl shards that made her sharp teeth electrify his hunger for the taste of deep kisses and cunt she promised once they exchanged vows.

in the neon chapel, the priest looked up quizzically at her hijab to pronounce "your people are my people" then continued a bit faster until she grinned the final "i do."

they chose a dingy motel. its stifling air surpassed the sadness of the marriage shop that should've been an altar where bodies symbolically begin to remerge as one whole and amorphous love. as such, the splotched and threadbare sheet over the hard, paper thin mattress where they lay naked at last might have been ground zero for lives of mutually assisted restructuring. but this never was because he couldn't get it up.

in this last year of their teenage, she already knew her patience only fueled his discomfort further. this had never happened to him and he thought her assurances that whole lifetimes lay ahead belittled the importance of his failure. how could he live any lifetime without the regular thrusts of muscle smashing the lead of his trusty wood?

the next day, he met a small street poet who had met goddess pele while hiking the black girth of smoldering kilauea alone. she led him up three flights to her studio overlooking the harbor. he felt calm as she pushed her door shut, for his wand had already stiffened. his comfort only increased as the night wore on, each wearing the other as they writhed and churned, playing plunge and plash with bodies none pledged to unite unless the rumbles of thunder drowning out the patter of raindrops hammering window and rooftop expressed the sardonic rite of impish trickster consorting with a wily, fluid priestess.

as dawn broke through the single window in that attic, two groggy adulterers reckoned the stiffy was almost more ready to replay than her soggy bottom. but not. it struck him: one of these three persons must be a witch. but which one?

billy come home makin a commotion like tarnation itself. we in the kitchen. at the stove, susanna stop stirrin chittlins. me and posey at the table — choppin it, laughin — we hush. we all three of us find billy sprawl out on his back on the porch. he head block the screen, foam out his mouth, he gurglin. kinda grinnin in a way it ain't laughin, crazy. susanna take one look and say, "we gone tie im to my bed. i'ma get my rifle, find the white buck. y'all feed im chittlin broth from the baster."

"hot?" posey ask.

"lawd, chile, no! let it cool!"

once we lift billy on susanna's bed, she sigh and muse, "i been wonderin why i'm buyin chittlins for easter. can't remember when i done it last. now i knows."

"i was wonderin, too," i say.

"i'm finna go now," susanna say. "got my conch. y'all listen up, best you can. i'ma blow it when i need posey help guttin the gall. meantime, y'all start some lye with the stove ash and crikwater." she look at me half stern for emphasis to tell me, "you gone hafta stay with billy. don't get skeered."

"yes, mam," i nod, already tremblin with the fears.

billy twitch like a cartoon monkey. he snurl and wail like a ruttin cat. he sweat pores open wide stank. mucous and foam drain out his mouth and nose in puddles. i shovel out some ash and sift it and boil water on the stovetop in the steel pot and mix the white ash in and scoop chittlin broth in the rice pot and let it cool while i dab and wipe his head with a couple washcloths i keep rinsin and wringin at the sink. mostly i'm scared to touch his skin with mines. and every time i feels the clammy boiling rubbery suck that's his brown skin turnin yellow against mines, i hear susanna say again, "don't be skeered!"

posey go when we hear susanna blow. they back home come sunrise. billy holl'in the whole time, say it's a woman bitin him, wild, black like lucy mare, strong haunches, hard feet, great titties, ripe cunny he like to fall deep in, ain't come out, terror he can't scream enough away.

"lye bout right," susanna say, "now this." and she scrape lye rusty yellow like apple cider out the pot, roll in the gall til it go hard. "hold the boy mouth open," susanna say, "don't let im bite you."

nightfall, he right like rain.

the anti-agent stared blankly at the apothecary without fixing his gaze on any one of the diverse tinctures and pondered the gravity of what it means to mature, to ripen, to rot, to grow up, or out of or into something or other or not, grow old, even. he was a long time standing there, still, stuck, stagnating because for every pondering there arose incalculable permutations of possibilities posing as answers pounding each other to dust. nonetheless, he elected not to take a powder in light of the fact that he needed to escape a cohort of pro-agents clamoring for blood just the other side of the moldy old walls.

the temple whore's chants fell on deaf ears, her flesh was a blur. despite his discontent with the content of anti-agent affairs he had abided and fomented for years, he was even more leery of the pro-agent program. that anyone should promote a thing insulted him. plus, he suspected that pro-agents were either very young and naive or very old and determined to meet death's weird goddesses with a happy face to help their entry to heaven or nirvana or other cloud cuckoo constructs of the utopiate addiction for betterness.

at least his fellow anti-agents veered with vim into the vast spectrum of plural perceptions that invalidated the narrow vanity of values. "if only there was a portal out of here into a realm not unlike this; one that recognized the incongruity of its impenetrably malleable tethers," he started to think before catching himself imagining a less dumb place more suited to what he already knew that he didn't. his time was running out of years, a twisting illusion that couldn't even own up to the reality of the illusory bc it wasn't.

maybe he would try the skin cream, submit to the yellow jar's call, its purple label. his eyes narrowly focused on it; tinctures evaporated, dried plants crumbled to dust, the floor sank, recomposing as if its decomposing wood fibers sought to rejoin the soily mycorrhizae from whence they came. but all this held to the illogic of causality, and he remained unimpressed when the skin cream screamed for what i scream: a good red whine and . . .

— *text breaks off here [ed.]*

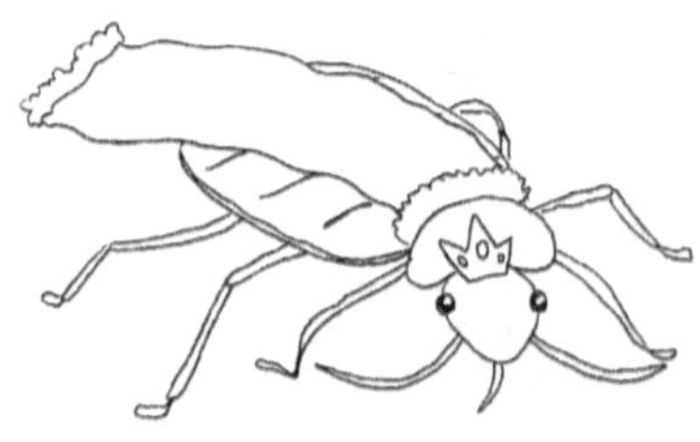

why should i put myself out there? people are mean. and scared. and i'm scared of em. i should know to keep my feelings to myself. no one ever offers me anything real. and all the love i gave away is gone. it's not like i can get it back. nothing will replace it.

my life is my business. what i do will stay secret. no one will know the reason. i don't care if anyone thinks i'm sensible or not. they don't believe a word i say. not one iota. every breath gets me nothing but senseless outcomes. all my efforts show me that my decisions are meaningless. what i do is for me. the reasons are best kept to myself. nothing can make me believe otherwise. i won't give another person power to disrupt my peace. i won't be at their mercy. it sickens me to hear all this phony talk of love. all they really want is to fight me, to hurt me more than i can even guess, then tell me it's my fault, my choice. and they're right. i won't be caught giving anybody anything just so i can lose. just to help them achieve the selfish ends that amount to nothing but my downfall and humiliation.

i'm special. i know this about myself and i'll defend what others don't recognize. i'm creative and what i do is better than all the lousy crap people appreciate. why defend the obvious? i hate how they think they know me. how could anyone be so stupid? no one knows me. i'm not the same as anyone. i need to find a way out of here.

there must be someone better. someone good. somebody above the swamp i see. somebody who's really real. if only i knew them. they must be out there. someone special who naturally sees how other people are "beneath" us. i thought that's how it was with tracy and then pedro and later, justine or octavia. but they all turned out to be weak, different from what i thought; from friend to frenemy to enemy. i can't believe i called them "friend." where are they now? i don't even know if they're in the world anymore. if they ever were.

no more illusions. no more dumb decisions. i'm just gonna take care of my body. it's the only thing that's worth it. i made mistakes. but i tried. i had good intentions. i gave and gave and gave. and what did i get back? nothing.

eighteen thousand acolytes from all corners of the kingdom converge at the summit, eager to further the search for whatever this is. the lineup of critters credentialed to address the crowd resounds with electric promise. i sit on papa's shoulders and as he and mama hold hands as if tethered, so do me and zxylvy, my wise and beautiful sibling.

not far from one of the many aquifers, the opalescence spilling through radiant new daylight over the dirt and dust so many feet cannot fail to trust replenishes the sweet breath released with the deep green of the young and old trees that have marched here to create such a welcoming grove. we must sing, our little clan's voices joining the rising chorus of crowing cocks and wakeful birds that arouse this animal conclave in ordinary mystery already veering adrift from its confusion of stated purpose. as if everywhere, the immediacy announced by a rumble of drummings the monkey sect starts for others to join rushes into the blood and prompts skin stretched round muscle to push and pull after the careening caprice of a cosmos in flux.

i am excited; rendered ever more vibrant by the meaningless squeals fired out the face of perfect zxylvy, a joyful explosion i don't care to resist until my own noises arise and are no longer mine. mama papa, too, are swept up inside and out, starting their own clamor with halting barks and tentative yelps that quickly evolve into the harmony of bodies opening all around.

and now, the drumming halts on a dime so the horde's harmolodic voicing subsides and the shamble of shamans invoking chaos from order parades across the distant circle of six stages arranged as a hexagon apparently hugging against the horizons.

"oop oop!" announces the hoopoe, flaunting the vertiginous vigor of its zebra-striped wings. "honor the ancestors by anointing your nests with human poop and lick the eyes of the old ones to share your warmth or die the death!!" decreed the bright bird. the agreement performed by the mass nodding of heads seems rightfully rhythmic, and our fam mimics this wildly.

"zuzzuzza, zuzzuzza!" declares the workabee, its five eyes aglow. "our children are common to all! our home is shared by all! the lands of our planet hold us all! our creative acts are the actions of all! our food is food for us all! our foraging flights are revealed to us all! our allegiance is honored by all and in honor of all! our queen is queen of the queen of all! zuzzuzza!" and the ensuing chorus of eighteen thousand zuzzuzzas assumes its own shape that holds all aloft a moment before its gentle dissolution returns us to the slow growth of gravity's grip.

many and more come the speakers appearing so to speak from the sweeping fields of phyla forming our fortress of flora and fauna: burdock and rose, condor and bobcat, muskrat and mugwort, poppy and panther, dolphin and birch, owl and oak and on and on address the throng through the ecstasy of word made phantom of fear and love. towers of flame stand as sentinels at the sides of the daises, pushing up. seemingly luminous, the robust scattering of countless fly-by-night firepits strive for the same hues of coral and copper, sparks coiling every which way. i half long for a torrential downpour, but the sky is a deep void of translucent blue, empty of clouds.

finally, the keynotes attain the central peak of a great crimson capped aminita muscaria. glistening slime from every pore, a pair of slugs engages in speechless and interlocking intercourse that involves all four of their personal pairs of privates. when they feel finished and fail to free their phalli from the other, each slowly and surely chews off these locked cocks, while an outspoken octopod reassures the assembly that procreation will proceed without stint for both of these hoary hermaphrodites.

"so you see," says mama assuming the mantel of sacerdote, "the organism is a portal of parthenogenesis that supplants in ecstasies the integral pain and death it involves with its bodies of trust."

"damn skippy!" chimes in papa from under the crown of hawthorne he's woven all day.

zxylvy bleats forth the happy laughter all kids carry and thrust and i have no option but to ape them just as a cobalt skinned battleship of nimbus anchors above the enthralled throng to open wide its vast hold of cascading rains.

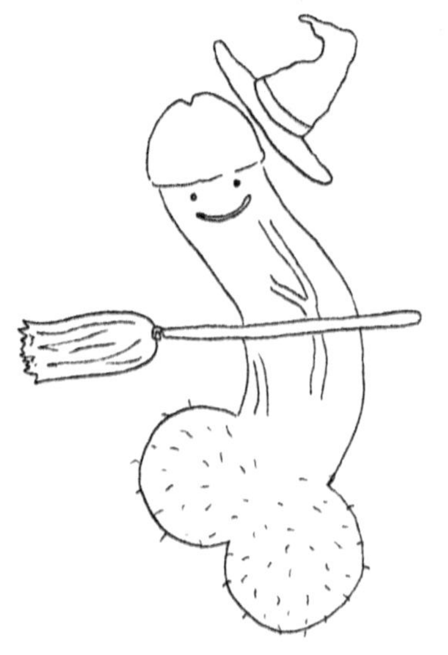

you remind me of the woman i love. or she reminds me of you. but you're not the ego i remind me of. and that's ok.

the woman i love, she comes and she goes and she gives me words and things and leaves things behind that she finds and calls hers even tho we both know that no thing is hers bc even if there were things and me and her then they would be ours but they're not bc that's not how this is. even tho i play along for the beauty of castoffs found and made as if renewed in the revolving of headspin and magical touch we plant in the darkness left by what shines us against the muscle and squish that trips the fantastic electrics extended magnetic as infinite stretches from nowhere who knows.

not that the woman i love takes anything from me because i have nothing to give having been here too long without being shipwrecked or cast up from the deep and knowing nothing worth having or winning or losing or why a knot will keep something to keep me from keep-looking to see if it's not. sometimes when still i will offer the woman i love unsolicited sounds from my mouth and squiggly lines out my fingers as if they are suitable for a woman i love who doesn't ask for them until she asks, whereon i spill them like beans behind everywhere clumsy as if nothing will grow healthy leaves i can climb on after she ascends out of my reach before i lose sight while i am holding my breath thinking the woman i love leaves me breathless.

and so i practice holding my breath for the woman i love the way i practice for me, knowing the woman i love is a mermaid and no man who can't hold his breath deep and long is worth the end that follows his finding the folly of loving a mermaid who hangs portals to life on land at the fake door of the room i remade the aquarium of a drowning escaped by hanging my effigy there until i snatched the belt tightened around my neck and cinched it to my waist as if i might really choke myself out for better or worse.

i hold my breath for the woman i love bc you remind me she is the mermaid i love who moves like the waves that are constant ripples that repeat without stint the waxing and waning and coming and going that flows us into the oceans that spawned air for spores spewed willy nilly to root like willow and hemlock and hawthorne the hoot owls have hidden amidst for a hundred million years that mean nothing to them more than the slow bunny fufu that's ready for lunch at the drop of a swoop from the heavens at night.

i hold my breath knowing i cannot stop the woman i love leaping for air as if a mermaid can breathe it by seizing control from the winds that bring breath like ships sailed closer to the cave where she flattens the tires that would let her lost sailors return to the land their old mothers saw fit to plant them on.

i hold my breath bc i want to stop the woman i love and hold her while knowing i cannot stop and hold the woman i love bc i hold my breath wanting to stop the woman i love and hold her.

i hold my breath because there's no failure for anything that i or the woman i love might mistakenly fail to do or not in our mutually brazen mistaken failed effort to tame the tangled trace of mermaidenhood she would prefer to arise from her breast like mother and babe unconditionally jesused as salvation from and of a land she never truly dared inhabit bc she could not if she tried with or without me, before, during or after.

i hold my breath therefore bc i do not need to hold my breath, not on land nor under the earth nor even within the waters she forgets are not hers alone — just like i, too, forget everything as if i could remember being reminded of the woman i love.

i can breathe underwater bc it is i who have made the woman i love the mermaid i love, for the woman i love never was the mermaid i love nor even the woman i love, as you know well if you've listened to me, you who are not the woman i love you remind me of just as the woman i love could never be nor remind me of the woman i love when it is i who made her the woman i love when i made myself love the woman i love who i never loved because i can only love the woman of love as i love who you remind me of loving, as if the woman i love i love bc she is no more and never was nor will be the woman i love. you see, the woman i love is nothing, like me.

Ariana finished her flute lesson with Mrs. McPherson and put the instrument in its case and gripped the handle and slung her backpack over her opposite shoulder and walked out the classroom door to skip down the hall part of the way to where Maya and Vicki sat outside on the school building steps playing cat's cradle.

"You guys wanna come swimming?" Ariana asked.

Vicki went slack-jawed and googly eyes at once. "Duhh," she said. "Whaddaya think we're waitin' for you for?"

There are eight million kids in the city and every one of them was at the Lucy Parsons Public Swimming Pool.

"Holy cannoli!" Ariana stopped in her tracks. "Is there even any water in there?"

"The first boy that touches me, I'm yelling rape," determined Vicki.

"I wouldn't if I was you," Maya warned.

"Whaddaya mean, Maya Papayovski? You're not me!"

"Suit yourself," Maya shrugged, "But I think you'll only incite the rest of 'em."

"She's got a point there," Ariana chimed in.

Vicki snorted and pointed her nose somewhere higher than its standard elevation. "The lifeguards won't let it happen, no way."

"Eight scrawny lifeguards versus four million horny wet boys?" wondered Ariana. "Good luck!"

"'Eight lifeguards,' my butt!" laughed Maya. "She means one! Carmelita Gonzales' big brother. I can't believe you're so in love with him!"

"Whaddaya mean?" Vicki was curiously at a loss for words.

"That guy has a new bae every week!" said Maya.

"Not to mention, he's ancient," Arianna added.

"He's not ancient!" Vicki protested. "When he's twenty-eight, I'll be twenty-one. . ."

"Yeah, well until you're eighteen and he's twenty-five, you ain't nothin' but jailbait to him, little girl!" teased Maya.

Vicki turned and faced Maya directly to lean back and point at her own shorts. "Eat me, Maya Papayabitch!"

"Vicki!" exclaimed a distressed Ariana looking left and right in chagrin. Fortunately, the swarm of striplings was occupied in a variety of other more immediate attentions. Vicki whirled her backside around to shake a tail feather at Maya, both of whom scrunched up their faces in combative expressions. "Are you guys gonna swim, or what?" refereed Ariana.

"Where the heck are we supposed to change?" Maya wondered. "There's only like three lockers on a normal day. Plus, look at that line. It's practically halfway to China!"

"I got my suit on underneath," Vicki said.

"Me, too," Maya conceded. "But what about our stuff?"

"I know, right?" agreed Ariana. "I don't care about my stupid books. But my mom'll kill me if some creep steals my flute. . ."

"None of these morons is interested in your six-hole stick, Nani," smirked Vicki.

"Good thing it has six holes instead of one on the end, or you'd think it was a blow-pop," Ariana retorted.

"Omigod, you guys!" Maya intoned. "Why's everybody got crabbypants on? Just stick the thing in your backpack and let's go in!"

"Okay, Maya Jenkins," Ariana wagged a forefinger, "but if one of these chickenheads steals it for a crackpipe, I'ma tell my mom it was you!"

"Same goes for me when I get raped!" Vicki chortled.

"By your dirty old man boyfriend?" Maya countered. "He's already a registered sex offender in twenty-three states, twenty-two countries, fourteen planets and ninety-nine galaxies!" She had shed her outer garments and was bounding for the poolside by the time she got out the last word and cannonballed into the water.

"Take it ba-aa-aaack!" squealed Vicki in barefoot pursuit before leaping in a very freestyle, limbs akimbo fashion into the drink.

Ariana stood as alone as possible in the swirling tempest of bodies blooming at full tilt. Her shoulders slumped, bookbag in one hand, flute case in the other. She squatted over both, watching her friends as she slowly and carefully snuck the case into the bag and zipped it up. She stayed hunched over that way for some time, silently mouthing, "Please, God, don't let them take my flute please," until she was satisfied she would never be satisfied with a definite answer, and all that would happen if she waited for one is that she would never go in the pool, even though swimming after her music lesson had pretty much been her idea since she got in bed last night and her mom told her to get some rest because today was gonna be a hot one. She sucked her tongue and stood up and half-dragged her bag to a spot close to the edge of the pool and set it down and took a breath and ran headlong for what looked like a gap in the waves.

Halfrabbit Halfdog

We saw each other every day and every night for years. I had a slew of names I called Lana: Lonnypants and Landrover and Lonnabonana and Lanipunani and Lankymaster and a thousand other things I came up with for no reason other than to keep smiling and laughing like fun was a crime and we were rebels without a care. Of course, we were so careless things turned reckless long before we both knew we had to be careful. I never said so and neither did she but you know there was other motherfuckers talking and making big shite.

"Fuck 'em," she said, and I said so too.

At a bonfire night outside town, Damien got loud about Lana. She stood up from the big log a bunch of other people were also sitting on passing whisky and weed. She said, "Fuck this shit!" and started for the house. Damien pointed at her and howled. When he stopped, an owl hooted from the trees standing round the edge of the big pond.

Bobby said, "Fuckin' owl." The coyotes got to yelping on cue, much farther away.

"Fuckin' coyoteeeeezz!!" roared Damien.

Lana stopped in midtrack and turned and yelled, "Fuckin' bitch! Fuck you! You fuck!"

Peepers and crickets and snap crackling wood was the only next sound. Then Marissa said, "Day-amn."

I found Lana in the kitchen in the house. A fire was glowing in the living room fireplace where Jasmine and Jake were making out and fingerfucking like teenagers do. I walked past and sat across from the bestie. "Motherfuckers," she said. "What the fuck?!"

I rubbed my eyes with the heels of my palms for

as long as it took to feel like my head felt different inside than when I started. When I stopped finally, Lana was looking at me quizzically and said, "What the fuck was that about?" on top of a swivel and crane of her neck for emphasis and added without missing a beat, "Is there any whisky?"

I shrugged at the same time as Jake must have come up for air in the living room to say, "You freeloaders better leave her parents' liquor alone! They'll be pissed."

Lana's jaw dropped and her eyes went saucer sized and probably her muscles got tight and then loose like a slingshot rubber band action, because she sprang out her seat after (it seemed) she crouched over Jake — Jasmine knocked outstretched cold on the oriental or Persian between the unkempt Ottoman and the dilapidated Davenport — looking like bleached blonde Vampirella from the back, the way her feet planted on his thighs. She curled her neck round the corner of his head and snarled and lunged and shook until she tore away and whipped her skull and tresses back to display a bloody chin under her toothy grin snapped fast on a gob of flesh like a freed harpy jackalope.

Jake keened like a banshee with one hand clapped over the bloody gushing and Landshark bounded out under the bright harvest halfmoon to wait at the car, where she spat the top chunk of his ear in her palm like it was pirates' booty: red and white blotch for me to see.

You can imagine it didn't end well with Jake's call to the cops and a knock on the door opening next morning to four uniformed and armed people between me and Jake's bandaged head. But Lana was never jailed and there is no end to our friendship of love, for, all these years later, tonight we are going out drinking again.

i remember the dream. nothing but the dream. all is invisible. you are not here. to believe that you are who you choose to be in the little place where you think you stand is to believe the impossible. i do not say that what you believe is wrong, but i do know that it is not possible. i know this because we all dream all the time and we dream without knowing why. we dream without knowing that what we see as real is but the dream we never awake from. i know this without any knowledge of what knowledge means. once, just yesterday — even tomorrow — everyone knew this. i told this to everyone because this was known when i told them the dream i will tell you.

nobody listened. no one would dance or sing or drum. this was no time for a woman's illusions, they said. they said this was a time for war. they didn't know that the white man they came to kill was already deep in their blood. i told them this and they laughed at me. they told me to touch their brown arms, to cut open their shoulders. they bade me to drink their thick purple blood.

i couldn't keep quiet. i told them this dream even after their backs were turned. i tell them now, even after their eyes, like mine, are long since meat for the crows. this is the time of dreaming. this is the land of our dreams. when we are dreaming, we are never awake. this is the dream.

a heavy silence smothered the forest. a stillness hardened sweet sap in the tree. hardened the people's blood to black. to stone. lake meecheeleemakeenak's waters had stiffened long before this, had turned to obsidian wrinkles clear to the vanishing point. i wanted to ask how such a thing came about. but the lodges stood empty and reeking of loneliness like ghosts of the eight winds huddled around the untended ceremonial fire, its golden tongues curled and trapped upwards in mid-lick, mimicking heat where no songs urged on no dancers, no drums rumbling the dustless dirt.

my unborn son — still nameless, so that i couldn't call him back, so that my tongue defied my will, my voice clogged in my craw — my unborn son — moist soil of my belly, not-yet-infant undaunted by blossoming fear or vainglory — my unborn son had pulled himself free like a skinned fawn quitting the brush-covered barbacoa pit — my unborn son had ambled away from our lodge to our shore, our entrails entangled in the umbilical tie from omphalos to diaphragm. atop and across the lake he continued. my unborn son, increasing in size with each crow-footed step, as if his flight toward a vanishing point brought him nearer my breast until the waters opened without warning and he plunged below without a cry. the crashing crowned waters' foamy splash, tall as a tidal, fell soft as a petal and spread no ripple. no wave sucking sound touched my ear.

at last, a croak fled my mouth's secrets — a startling bark, the death rattled yelp of a dog hanging high and nose-down from the broad crest of a manitou totem. i felt melting in my bones, a sluggish flow like beached sand washing upwards inside the rising length of a catalpa trunk, slow-burned to hollow. i could turn my head only to hear the rasp of knives' teeth honed against each other as i did so. caring for nothing but the well-being of my gargantuan unborn whelp, i moved away from the midst of the emptied wikiwams towards the lake's edge on all fours — not on my palms and knees; but with my knuckles dusting the earth, my bare soles slapping topsoil, a three-legged coyote pup miming a crab.

the waters receded in time as i neared the

desolate shoreline. at some far distance, this slippage increased until a towering wave menaced all the land with its faceless maw spitting forth a roar like barrels of laughter, deafening as the niagaras' great falls. knowing i should tremble, i couldn't. my flesh prickled like a plucked guinea hen. just so, i reached into the exposed gut of the waxing upsurge, certain of setting my hand to that of my lost and unknown son. of an instant, i felt a warm and boneless flesh and guessed his soft bottom greeted my grasp instead. and now the waters collapsed upon my brittle back with a tremendous crack i feared spoke like a splintering stone sistered to the anvil of gravity. fish i had never allowed in nevertheless escaped my mouth in schools of choked and deadened colors. their rank scales tore up my tongue. beaver's cub attached to my teat, mistaking it for a stump, gnawing and suckling it to bursting over and again.

even as blisteringly fat leeches gorged at my eyes — blind with gore — i knew the soft skin squeezed in my fingers' grip was no boy... i gripped the medicine bag of crane, threaded with beads and shells, feathers and fishbone. out of this spilled such a quantity of cracked arrowheads scratching the broken teeth of lost warriors that the slivers sliced the bloodsuckers wide. my eyeballs opened, free to watch the water now fallen up to my waist. displaced by the heft of this fluid heap, petrified by this outpouring, my mouth took dry and my tongue swelled and gorged it as i fought to cast away the bag of bad medicine — no longer crane's — tearing the skin from my hands with each futile thrust. it refused to go, smothering the entire landscape with its sun-bleached shards of cut stone and jawed bone until the tremendous figure of Antoine Laumet de la Mothe, Sieur de Cadillac, strode with hunger wolf's lope straight for me. his pale, hair-nosed snout stopped a thumb's breadth from my cheeks. a foul air crept out his every pore so that i longed to gag. i struggled, scarcely able to squirm against the mutating blob growing into my depleted root. the howling emitted from Cadillac called down a plague on the life of all that is born of the very earth, and a withering seized up my well-being, deep within. was this fear or surrender? i cannot say. neither did i find reason for the shame and the weakness, the fatigue and the blind, shabby rage that glutted me.

if ever i have hated, this was the moment that every hate i have known boiled and baked me inside on out. a foreign void of familiar traces sprouted a field of echoes deep in my skull to summon the night's loneliest horny mare to push her gleaming jet back between my cut naked thighs. unbidden, she bolted and whisked us away just underneath the solid terrain of tooth and shale. the bloodless leer of undead Chief Cadillac hovered, unnerving me, steady and constant and close, my legs clenched tightly astride the black mount's bulging back muscles, my whitened knuckles enmeshed in her jet mane.

and now my tongue sliced out my lips, slithering as it stretched ever longer, scratching to shreds atop the rugged garden of jagged rock and splintered teeth. Chief Cadillac vomited, loosing a whisky geyser into every opened gash to split the length of serpentine muscle rearing up from the back of my gullet. a searing loosened my mind to a piercing bowel-sickness and a dizzying inability to focus on any one thing in any direction, near or far. still, i saw the pebbled expanse darken ahead, for the invisible mare of night charged ever faster, my middle tattered and gushing skin and scarred scalps. i was buffeted by a blustery biting from the sixteen points of a busted compass that screamed a cackling willful enough to knock me flat.

spirited headlong through the gloom on a dreary plain, i made out the flayed and eviscerated carcass of every imaginable creature of wood and stream, mountain and vale, large and small. here lay Coyote and Eagle, Sparrow and Hawk, Headless Owl and Elk, Pheasant and Frog Hewn In Two, Turkey and

Cricket Hacked To Bits, Salamander, Crow, Caribou, Badger, Hummingbird and too many more to mourn. finally, i saw under the mushrooming pile of pelts left to rot — where even Fly and Maggot and Ant numbered among the atrocity's lifeless objects — the expired bodies of Fox warriors, their vermillion masks ruddy with clotted blood; a busted nahuatl — a spirit animal — just out of reach of each of their severed hands. ruined by the witness through which i seemed to race like a wraith, i strained to shriek. instead, my tongue, leagues long and shredded, turned around of its own and snatched my throat, strangling away my life. Cadillac's omnipresent face opened his mouth wide enough to swallow the sky and commanded me in a voice that stopped everything all at once. spooked, the nightmare threw me free of its back, launching me into the breach, "Dee pah!" i knew these syllables to mean — without my understanding — either, "say nothing!" or, "ten steps!"

i landed in the huron and ottawa dance circle, its fire burning while one after a next of the howling, gyrating believers in our destruction each cut a chunk of purple bubbling flesh from my body. lumps of meat turned into Twin-Tail Coyote and White Biting Eagle, Bone-Hearted Sparrow and Silver Running Hawk, Flame-Breasted Little Owl and Stone Skipping Elk, Oak Nested Pheasant and Prairie Digging Frog, Hungry Horned Turkey and Eight-Legged Cricket, Beaver-Tailed Salamander, Three-Eyes Yellow Crow, Caribou Speaking Sky, Toothless Standing Badger, Snakeskin Barked Hummingbird — all meskwaki warriors with faces twisted and bewildered, rattled and rapidly dying.

and here, i awoke encased in a layer of icy cold rivers of pregnant mother sweat from the roots of my scalp hairs to the root that joins a body's hips to the soil. and here, i shudder against the laughing frost that creeps through muddy blood toward onrushing dawn.

— *transcription ends here.*
from an interview with Spotted Willow Fox,
19 april 1752, fort detroit [ed.]

NEW YORK
SOME GUY
DOB: 6/9/169
6'9" 169LBS

Male Order

The Blast is made out of the same brick as the high school, but it's only two stories with no windows and the walls painted gray under the graffiti we scrawl along Pine Street and back in the alley where the bands and the beer come in. The Blast is the only place we can go to hear hardcore and hang out without morons and punkbashers screwing around. Course, there's always a few skinheads, but you can handle them once they get used to you some. You can get in the Blast if you have no ID, but the bartenders are real strict about serving and none of the older kids wants to see the place busted over some squirt trying to get tight. A lot of people even say the cops are paid to stay away, which is fine with us. All that makes no difference, since we always find someone to buy for us before we get there. So, we either get cocked on the way or sneak in pints and halves and slug away crouched close to the floor in some corner or the middle of the wheel. The wheel is where you crash and burn. Kids are skanking or doing the worm or just rocking. Sometimes you get beaned by a dive or someone gets too drunk or stoned and it's a mess of puke all over and the floor is not big. I get loco for the wheel. I mean, I just love it. All the black and rags flap by, palefaces and fists and terror in the eyes, sometimes splots of blood might be yours but you know there is no telling 'til the next day.

Rich is five years older than me. I met him a couple years back when I first started hanging out at the Blast and drinking. Noel was my best friend back then instead of Sully, who is my best friend now. Rich would buy for me and Noel back then no problem, a lot of the time turning us onto pot. People say Rich was a great basketball player as a freshman. He never said much about it. We never asked. They say the coach asked Rich to be captain of the junior varsity team his sophomore year. He never showed for the tryouts. Not that I blame him. For all I care, you can take all the stupid sports and drive them a long way off a short pier as they say. I guess this was a big drag for Rich, though, everyone starting to call him a faggot just because he refused to jump around the gym trying to put this stupid ball in some hole twice his height from the floor. People will call you a fag for all kinds of senseless reasons. People call me a fag sometimes just because I dress a little different. Not people really, but rednecks and jocks and assholes like that; the black kids will laugh because to them, punk means fag. I just ignore the whole army of idiots, unless they get in the way.

The thing that is sort of embarrassing is that Rich did more than just buying for me and Noel. I can never remember how it got started -- I must have blocked it out of my memory -- but when there was nothing else to do and we were hanging around Rich's place, sometimes we would give each other head. That was a couple years ago, like I said, and not something I really like to talk about. I feel like I should, though, since people say that anyone could be queer and that you should never feel like anything is wrong with it if you are or if your friends are. My mom swears I have homophobia, but she has no idea what went on back then. Well, maybe she does, but even if she did know, and maybe since it did happen, I would never say I was homophobic. On the other hand, even though it did happen, I would never say I was a homosexual either. But only because I'm not.

The weird part about what me and Noel and Rich did was that I never looked at it as being queer or homosex or anything. I mean, I never talked about it or looked forward to it or anything. We just did it. We talked about the kinds of girls we thought were good looking and how we wanted to screw them and Rich would tell us about girls he met or went out with or balled or whatever. But at some point, he would always start it off by straight asking us if we wanted to do it, just like that, "You guys wanna do it now?" And we would just say yeah. Then we would do it in some kind of order with two of us going at it while the other guy read a comic book by himself or maybe even watched kind of detached like and then we switched after the first guy would nut and go like that 'til it was over with all three of us kind of satisfied, so to speak. It was all pretty normal, like masturbation, except there was somebody else with you. Like the way you toss off, you just cum and forget about it. That was how it was with these guys. When we finished, we would go on talking or drinking or smoking pot and listening to Rich's stereo like nothing ever happened.

One day when Rich gave me a ride home, my mom was coming up the sidewalk in front of our house. She looked at us and got this look on her face like she wanted to talk but forgot how, like if you have a nightmare and try to scream but don't and when you wake up it turns out to be too late. I got out the car, an old convertible Corsair with the top down on account of it being one of those beautiful spring days that gets everyone so delirious and happy go lucky. Rich drove off without being introduced and when I said hi to her, my mom right off asked me who he was. I told her it was Rich and then for some reason I got all embarrassed about everything with Rich and Noel. To change the subject, I asked where she was coming from, which was obviously the market, as she had two brown paper shopping bags in the little rolling handcart. She tried to act normal, but I could tell she was uncomfortable as I was. When she got the door open, I took the cart from her, and on the way upstairs, she asked me the regular questions about school and what I did after to which I gave the normal answers, like saying school was stupid and after school I did nothing. She told me to put away the groceries and went to her room to yak on the phone, for which I was grateful. As soon as I had the kitchen put away,

I split to my room and pretended to read 'til dinner. What I really did then was decide that this threesome of me and Rich and Noel was for sure too weird to keep going. Mom never mentioned Rich again, but it was a little uptight between us at dinner that night. In the morning, though, things were back to normal.

The next time I saw Rich was about a week later, and he never asked if I wanted to mess around or anything. It was like he knew I would say no. The whole time, he just bitched about money. He was selling too little pot to make his unemployment worthwhile. He was bummed out that he might have to work. Rich had his bass in his lap like he was about to play it, but he never did. When he ran out of things to say, he would pluck at the strings, nervous-like, but not playing really. We smoked hell of reefer, and when I split he gave me a joint he said was laced with heroin. I took it over to Noel's and we puffed it up and made like elephants on a goofball kick all afternoon. I never told Noel how I had enough of the messing around, but he seemed to figure it out, too.

* * *

It was around that time I started to go out with Collette Smith. I hung around her because she loved to make out and, to be honest, I never did it before, so I decided she would be a good way to learn. She already had a reputation, but when I told Rich about it, he said to forget about the kids at school. He said not everybody gets a reputation but everybody gets laid sooner or later, one way or another, like it or not. He said I would be lucky and I should be thankful if Collette let me do it with her. He bet that would give me a head start on almost everybody in my class. Besides, he said, if she let me do it, she must like me, since girls hardly ever do it with guys they hate. Me and Collette broke up after only a couple months, though. I guess I should say she broke up with me one day when I called her a slut for no good reason. I told her I was only joking and I hardly meant it but she knew all about that reputation and what the other kids said about her and saw through my lame excuses like reading a comic book. She told me she was nothing to joke about.

By the end of that little affair, I almost never saw Rich and I was so sick of the secret that I totally avoided Noel, even in the cafeteria. Rich might see me with some friends at the Blast or in the park and ask if we needed drugs or anything but I would say no right off, even if we were looking. This happened lots of times, 'til one time I was with Sully and Garth. They got riled up at me, asking what the hell was my problem. I told them Rich was a fag, that once he asked me for a blow job. They laughed and asked me if I did it. I lied and said I never sucked anybody's pecker and that nobody never sucked mine. Garth wanted to know what about Collette. I ignored him and Sully asked what my beef was with Rich if there was no dick-licking going on between us; if a guy says he can get booze or dope, it makes no difference if he does the bufu or not. Anyways, he said, if he ever asked us to do it, we could kick his ass or get somebody else to do it, turn him over to some rednecks or jocks.

So, Rich started to buy for us again. I mostly hung with him and Sully. Noel never came around and we never talked about him and there was no funny stuff. Rich really was okay and had dynamite drugs he gave us mostly for free. He was no sissy, either, and he went out with this beautiful super skinny girl from Pawtucket named Mary. She only has two years on me, and when she was going with Rich, she would scratch my head all affectionate and monkey-like and kiss me a sweet goodbye right smack on my mouth when she left with him. I sure liked her.

Sully made jokes about Rich and Mary, but only if we were someplace without them, and I laughed with him a lot, sometimes making jokes myself. We even called Rich "The Fag" behind his back, but it was really mostly sour grapes that he had the experience and Mary the beautiful girl and all.

* * *

What happened was that Rich got way stoned one night at the Blast right after Halloween and went back with Mary to her mom's house in Pawtucket. Mary says they started to fight over some petty disagreement and he got nasty, telling her she was nothing but a scrawny little wretched dyke fag hag. She told us it was only because Rich was so tight that he acted like that. He never was so mean as that as long as she could remember. There were times he might act like she was ignorant, like she bugged him some, but she figured all people got impatient with each other eventually, especially as they always hung out together. Anyways, Rich was loud and raging to the point of busting things up. Mary told him to get the hell out and he starts bawling, kind of like howling she said. Tears begin to fall and he cringes to his knees by the door, weaker than anybody she says she has ever seen, except her mom the day her dad split. This got Mary pretty scared so she told Rich to stay, but he kept saying no, no, and she was saying yes, yes, it was okay, 'til he finally got up and bolted out the door, down the stairs, out into the empty Pawtucket night street.

Mary tried to call Rich on the phone all night, but he never came home, and not the next day or the day after that. When she got him at last on the fourth day, he told her how he decided to walk off the weirdness after their fight, and he was almost home when the cops picked him up outside City Hall. A lot of fags hang around there late at night and the cops figured Rich was one of them and kept on calling him faggot, punk as they drove him out to India Point Park by the water over in the Portuguese neighborhood. They beat hell out of him. (The cops.)

Mary told us this one night at the Blast after there was no sign of her or Rich for about three weeks. She said Rich was three nights in the hospital and then he was afraid to leave home. He told Mary not to visit. She said he said he was sorry for going off that night and the reason he said he did it was not so much that he was high or tight as he was just a coward and a fag, which everybody knew just looking at him. And he said him and Mary should just face facts and give up on going out. He even said to her he knew me and Sully thought he was a fag and we were right, and we should hardly feel bad to see the truth he was too chicken to admit. Me and Sully felt sorry and bad about all this, and when Mary left we agreed we never should have called Rich "The Fag" so much and what a cool guy he was, and that we would miss his advice and of course all the drugs, too.

We saw Mary at The Blast all that winter. She had no more news from Rich. Sully would look at Mary and tell me how bad he wanted to do it with her. I told him to go ahead and go for it but he never did. We stopped calling her a dyke behind her back. I guess because with no Rich there was no more sour grapes. I kept quiet about how I wanted to do it with Mary. Sully and me were best friends now, and he probably had an idea of what I thought about Mary, even though I never mentioned it. I liked her a hell of a lot. It was a kick to see her change the colors of her hair or come around with some old new rags that kept her looking like a hobo. Mary is the coolest girl hanging at The Blast but, of course, justice would have it that she goes to another school. Still, we can be down there and I just love to watch her go and crash all crazy into the spinning wheel of the pit, her arms all gyrating and wild, crawling up over heads and shoulders on stage, first rolling on, then she skanks through the band with a face like this wicked four year old when she dives in the whirl of black and white and jeans.

I can be all burned from the last jam and head beat up tired to the push and shove ring outside the spin and slams in the mosh, and she goes and takes over, better than me, cooler. And sometimes, she'll scream in my ear, Watch this! and go deck some backwoods skinhead or dive right in the face of some obnoxious Nazi punk.

* * *

It turns out one day I was home reading Edgar Allen Poe when Mary calls to tell me how bored she is and I should come over. She said her mom got a bunch of new records from New York and we could listen to them together. It was so cold all week, I actually had to think about whether or not to face the outdoors. But her idea sounded good enough so I asked my mom for a few bucks and headed out into the North Pole.

The walk from the bus to Mary's practically froze my ears, fingers and toes for long term preservation and I was glad to get inside her house. Mary made tea and I suggested we should raid her mom's liquor to put some rum in it so we did. We turned on the Japanese horror movie from the UHF channel out of Boston but kept the sound off to hear these great records. I told Mary her mom bust be a swell lady to cop such excellent material. She said her mom knew everything good and a lot of weird, unknown shit, too. Her mom was going with some guy from New York who taught at RISD. He came to town in the middle of the week and then her mom would go to New York on weekends and check him out.

Mary explained she and her mom were more like sisters. That made me wish my mom was more into what I like, instead of all her weirdo friends always talking about correct action and kharma and bogus stuff like that. They always start blubbering on about how this thing I get into is negative and that I should say this wacky Buddhist chant, namyorangyko or something. As far as what I am into being negative, I never even claimed I was into anything at all. Besides, it seems pretty twisted to get all hung up on the right thing to do when every day the whole world is blowing up and dying right before our eyes. I just go to my room or split the house altogether when too many of her dippy freaks come around.

Then, me and Mary got on the subject of drugs. We both agreed drugs are the best way to expand the mind, wishing there was some way to get morphine or heroin or opium so we could try that like Lou Reed and Jim Carrol and Edgar Allen Poe used to do. That led us to planning a trip to New York, where you can get anything you want anytime, which somehow got us on the sex topic. Mary told me about her first girlfriend, this black chick from her school. She said they met walking home one day and this girl invited Mary to her house. She got Mary in the bedroom to look at this photo album and the next thing was they were making out. She went down on Mary, which I guess was freaky at first, but Mary said she got to really like it and she even did it back. She said this went on about six months but this other girl played these games and stood Mary up a lot. Mary really liked her and she said they never really broke up, just sort of drifting apart.

Of course, now Mary asked me if I ever did it with boys, and I felt the sweat under my arms and my body get hot and I lied. I was hoping Rich kept his mouth shut but naturally, he had told her everything. She said it was okay. She liked me, she said. Then she kissed me and unzipped my pants and started playing with it so that before I knew why, we were naked and I was blushing because I finally lost my virginity to a girl. Mary was super nice the whole time and kept asking was I okay and I said yes, or if I was nervous and I said no and she giggled. I tried to get on top to do it like missionaries, but she ended up on top of me and I did not last very long at all. I was totally embarrassed but she kept on kissing me lots, telling me I was a beautiful boy, and she moaned so much and loud enough I got scared and wondered did I hurt her. It was a neat thing with Mary, not like Rich and Noel. I guess I had thought a lot about it instead of it just happening, even though I never believed it would, and it did sort of just happen. But it was cool. We held close a while as the record ended and the Japanese dragon movie turned into kung fu.

When we got up, Mary heated a pot of chili her mom left on the stove. We watched Apocalypse: Now! on cable, eating a few bowls of chili, a bag of Fritos and some more rum. When the movie ended, we went to The Blast in a delirious head, making noises and faces at each other, dancing and skipping or walking too slow and too fast through the cold, empty winter night. We just leaned on each other that night, all quiet for a long time, then talking excited like we never did before between the rudies and hellatious rock -- Bad Brains in town -- sneaking the softest kisses in the shadows, almost kisses like rushes.

Mary and me kept this up all winter, and it looks like we maybe made it to summer, even though I feel a little bored. The way it goes is, in winter, the cold made it hard to hang out too much. Weekends we ended up at Mary's and a lot of my Fridays in school were a big waste, as I would be thinking all day about going to her house to do it. Since spring came, we hang in the park a lot. Sully is with us more and me and Mary are pretty used to each other. We can probably go through summer and then figure out whether to go at the new year with a clean slate or what.

The problem with a girl is she keeps you from hanging with the guys you like and you get this dependency routine going, even though you were doing fine before you met her, or at least you think you were. I guess I forget how bad I wanted her to start with. So, the other side is it can be just as big a drag to be with the guys all the time when all they do is talk about girls like a big peacock parade or how much cash they can get doing this or that or the big silly business of trying to smoke the most pot or drink the most. So, Mary and I go on, even though I know she wants to be by herself a lot more, reading her books and writing her poems, while I go cross-eyed trying not to look at some other girl, or just wanting to escape on some great big old clipper ship to a thousand years ago, like in the song.

* * *

One of the first spring days, when all the people are into this big phony smiley culture everywhere you go -- pastel and white and RayBans and automatic cameras in Providence, for Christ's sake -- me and Mary headed for the park after school and thankfully, it was not too crowded, just a bunch of greasers in their mondo-mobiles over by the zoo. Sully was waiting over by Roger's big empty famous yellow house and lit up a zombie joint that only started to hit us fifteen minutes after we complained it was beat. Right as I started to feel burnt, here comes Rich in smelly black leather with no shirt on and he sits just by Mary. He was smoking a joint he handed to her and asked if we wanted to cop some acid. Right away he pulled out this pistol that scared shit out of us, but we stayed cool like they say if a dog is after you and for a minute I wondered was it real, too chicken to ask. He pulled the clip out to look in the hold and then down the barrel before dropping in two bullets and shoving it back in. I was amazed at how huge and black and shiny it was, like some movie piece, and the bullets had these ugly pointed ends I would not want to be in front of for anything. Rich went on about the acid, how good it was, said he just took thirteen hits. Then he offered some to us free since his money was taken care of. "I live on this shit and it's damn good for ya. Been takin' it everyday for a month now and it's the best shit in the world." He raised his eyebrows, waiting for our answer. We shook our heads, no, like our mouths were glued by the paste the reefer made of our spit.

Rich was oblivious to our answer, just rubbing at the gun with a rag like he thought it was some magic lamp with a genie inside it waiting for his command. Mary and I were not holding hands and we shimmied our thighs apart to make it seem like we were not making out as much as we were. It seemed like forever we sat in the too quiet shadows of Roger Williams' big old house there in the park. I was tempted to ask Rich for some acid, not knowing what else to do, but my imagination was wild with all the horrible things he could do with the gun: rape us, kill us, all the terrorist torture you ever saw on the news or read in the papers or movies. So I figured the acid would only be worse and forgot about it.

Rich never said another thing until he stood up kind of mechanical, like one of those toys in that scientist's shop at the end of that movie about the replicant hunter. He stuck the gun in his jacket and walked down the hill, complaining what a bunch of little kids we were. When he was a good way, he stopped to look back like he left something. "Come on!" he yelled. We just sat there. He walked all the way back to us and stood all hazy a minute and then stared right at me. "Fuck you if I am a faggot, motherfucker." He was quiet for a couple minutes, just standing there like he liked making us all nervous and then he said, "You know my name, look up my number." That was when he left for good. We felt all ashamed and said nothing until I decided to joke about how hard Rich was tripping, saying he was tripping so hard he would fall up instead of down if he tripped on something else. We were stoned and dead anxious to forget what just went down, so my not very funny joke got us laughing real easy.

At first, me and Mary agreed this gun was Rich's way of scaring us, letting us know he was not so keen on us going out. We talked about breaking up for a while or not seeing each other so much or at least hiding out, but we decided there was nothing to do if Rich wanted to kill us. It would be chicken to call the cops, since even though Rich was acting crazy, he was still a cool guy, and especially not after what the pigs already did to him. I think me and Mary had a little bit of a death wish, too. Or the idea of going on with normal life had this extra suspense in it or tension, like all of a sudden now we were big Spanish dictators or mercenaries or something.

It only took a couple more times seeing him to let us know Rich was not pissed at us at all, or if he was, we were not his major problem. Rich had obviously gone a little whacked in the head. He came around to lecture us on how evil people are, how kids used to pound on him, burn him with cigarettes and matches, kick him down stairs, shove him in dumpsters or toilets. There was this huge list of all the ways Rich was messed with right up until dropping out of school a month before graduation. He said he hated society because society hated him, so there was no point to graduating. If all the assholes thought one month of school made such a big difference, then he said they were stupid and he did not need them to begin with. He hated politicians and big businesses and society. He kept saying everyone was a hypocrite, even him. He made all these speeches to us sitting hunched over the gun, staring at it, polishing it, spitting on it or on the ground at his feet. Sometimes he would spare us the speeches and just sit there muttering, "Fuckers, they won't fuck me." Just like that, over and over.

* * *

I was in the school cafeteria on another of those golden happy joy-joy days when everybody acts like the Pepsi company is paying people major bucks to smile. Right outside the window, the prom king and queen are making out like the Breakfast Club Star Search finals, when I see Rich walking over the plaza with his gun. I doubt most people saw the gun at first, but by now I had a habit of looking for it whenever Rich came around. He usually had it, too. Of course, that was always at the park and he never came around the school. There was no reason for him to be there.

Rich came right into the cafeteria, pointing his gun at the old man security guard and a couple of teachers standing by the entrance. Everyone backed away slow with their hands up. No one screamed, but there were gasps and some kids made it out the room. Most of us stood around and watched Rich pacing with his right arm out and the pistol tight in his fist. He pointed it at people, but he never pulled the trigger. Once, Rich let the gun brush through Cindy Hunt's white hair and she went stiff as a board. Some people said later she shit in her pants, but I don't blame her. It was then Rich stopped to polish the gun a second, but only a second. He went to pointing it at people's heads now, yelling out, "Fag? Who's a fag?!" His eyes started blinking all wild-like and his face was tight so he looked mad as hell. This only went on maybe a few minutes like they would never end, and then the old man security guard got out his gun, like remembering his job, and he followed Rich around the room. He kept aim on Rich but never fired, since I guess he was afraid it might ricochet or something, but he sure looked like he wanted to be a hero and do it.

It was not long before Rich sat down and, when he did, he put that pistol smack at the center of his own forehead. At the top of his lungs, he screamed out, "BANG! BANG! You're dead! Fifty bullets in your head!" And then he started in this nutty laugh. He let his arm drop so the gun rested in his open palm on the table. That was when all the last of the kids started leaving. A lot of us were slow about it and I hung back way longer than just about anybody else, even though it was not on my mind to help out at the time. I was fascinated like the rest, and probably a little relieved to be out of there.

Rich kept the security guard away until the cops came in full force, like fifty of them with shotguns and rifles and nightsticks and bulletproof vests and walkie talkies and some of them had on riot helmets and some others were wearing hats from that old SWAT team show. They got Rich surrounded easy, and he kept turning round and round with one hand on the gun and the other on his wrist, the way he must have seen in Dirty Harry, never pulling the trigger and mumbling something no one could understand. And then, Rich got all contorted in his face and his body and started singing this song,

> Well, I asked a young policeman
> if he'd only lock me up for the night.
> Well, I had pigs in the barnyard.
> Some o' them, they're all right.
> Then he fucked me with his truncheon
> and his helmet was way too tight."

And then he started yelling the refrain, absolutely batshit,

> Wait'll I get my cock sucked!
> Wait'll I get my ass fucked!
> Yeah, I ain't got no money,
> but I know where to put it every time!

I doubt the cops were able to appreciate this little bit of Rolling Stones trivia, and a bunch of them rushed Rich and threw him on the ground as he got out the last words, "I'm a lonesome schoolboy in your town." We all heard his head smack the floor and there was this big weird sigh when it did, and then they cuffed

Rich and beat him wicked bloody and carried him off to jail.

Sully was in his class during that lunch period and even though I told him all what happened after he heard the rumors flying around, we never really talked about what it all means. I guess the reason you have a best friend is so there can be somebody you can avoid talking to about some things and still understand each other. As soon as I got home, I called Mary to fill her in. Later on , I went to her house from where I called my mom and lied to her that I was staying over Sully's. After a major phone battle, she gave in and I ended up in front of the tube with Mary and a pizza. Sully came by and we hit the rum, but he wanted to make The Blast before closing, so he split around ten. It was a jittery, nervy night, the three of us sitting there real quiet, like waiting in the emergency room for some mangled friend.

* * *

None of us knows whether Rich will get a trial or put in the crazy house or what. I keep avoiding the gossip at school, but I sometimes overhear things. All of it is usually a pointless crock of predictable idiocy from your hopeless high school needlebrains. Every now and then, some total no-mind will actually come up to ask if my girlfriend didn't used to screw that zany faggot who came to the lunchroom, and some of them even say they heard I was sucking his cock, too. I just tell them to fuck the hell off and leave it at that, otherwise I would end up in fights all day long. I just hope people are more intelligent when I leave this dump.

The Man, the King,
the Girl and the Spider

"I'm king!" yelled Paul, triumphantly poking a branch half his size and stripped of its bark by the elements up toward the treetops.

"I wanna be king!" Betty said, stepping closer to the fallen trunk where Paul stopped gesturing to look down at her.

"I have the sword, Excelsior!" he argued.

"You can't be king," Ruben said to Betty, "You're a girl."

"Girls can be king, too!" challenged Betty.

"No they can't!" sneered Paul, pointing the stick at Betty's face while she stared menacingly back.

"You can be queen," Ruben explained.

"No she can't!" screeched Paul, rearing back to glare at Ruben. "I have Excelsior and I have the power!" He held his head high.

"Actually, it's Excalibur," said Ruben.

Paul's grip on the stick tightened even as the rest of his body slumped. His jaw slackening, he studied Ruben a moment before reassuming command, "I don't have your stupid Ex-crapper or whatever you call it, scally-wag!" He wielded his stick with a wild deftness bordering on prosthesis. "My! Sword! Is called!" He took a big breath and proclaimed, "EX - CEL - SEE - OORRRR!!" After he finished crowing, he started swinging the stick anew, accompanied by whooshing sounds of varied intensity to help the air behave as he wanted it to do.

Betty and Ruben watched until Paul felt almost out of breath, at which point he struck the end of his stick on the trunk under his feet and puffed out his chest.

"Wow-oo," said Betty after a long silence observed — it seemed — even by the birds and the breeze-catching insects. "So, you're like one of those mad kings."

"Silence, incident woman!" barked Paul. He pointed his finger at her this time.

"What are you talking about?" Betty scrunched up her face like she'd bitten an unpeeled orange.

"He means 'insolent' woman," said Ruben.

Paul turned on Ruben with renewed zeal, shouting, "Guards! OFF with his head!"

"Did he not take his meds?" Betty asked Ruben.

"Wench!" Paul's face reddened with each breath and he thrust the branch back and forth in a manner that didn't quite support his voice. "I ordered you to be silent! Do you want to die with this ... scoundrel — " The word sent Paul into a fit of laughter, as if he surprised himself by using it, and he could barely finish his sentence, " ... on ... the ... ... guillotine ... " He continued to crack up, doubling over until he was on his knees and let go of his branch.

Ruben and Betty looked from Paul to each other, then back at Paul. "Okay," sighed Ruben while Paul indulged in his manic spasm until it morphed into a dramatic pantomime. "So, you're king of France ..." Paul widened his eyes and twisted his mouth open at this but said nothing, now clearly happy to explore his mime skills, "but you don't have any guards or executioner to carry out your orders. Plus, not to mention we didn't actually even agree to play Kingdom. When we left your house, we said we would decide what to play when we got here. But then, as soon as we did, you grabbed that stick and jumped on that tree and went nuts."

"I know! Right?" said Betty. "You're totally acting like you need a doctor or something."

"Ha!" scoffed Paul, returning to the spoken world. "We can't even play Doctor anymore, thanks to your big mouth."

"Shut up, Paul Googlysnotty!" snapped Betty. "I told you he promised not to tell!"

Paul leapt to his feet and snatched up his branch, wielding it like a baseball bat, "Betty Bedbug," he countered, "I swear to God — !!"

"Come on, you guys," Ruben refereed, "Are we gonna play Kingdom? Or what?"

"I'm king!" Paul yelled.

"I know you are but what am I?" teased Betty.

"You're the stupid girl," Paul said nastily.

"Okay, okay," said Ruben. "I say we make Betty queen."

"No friggin' way!" Paul whined. He dropped his stick and pouted with great effort. "I'm goin' home."

Ruben said, "C'mon Paul, why you wanna ruin it for everybody?"

"I'm not ruinin' nothin'!" hollered Paul. "Your ugly girlfriend is! I gave you guys PB and graham crackers AND chocolate milk!"

"Your mom made it for us," said Betty.

"At least — Yeah … well, she didn't feed us shit like your mom woulda, Bedbug!"

"PAUL!" exclaimed Ruben. "What the heck's bugging you? Let's just play Kingdom! Okay? You're king, Betty can be fortune teller, and I'll be the man called the Hand. And we all have to work together to defeat the evil monster no one's ever killed."

"No one can kill it?" Paul almost gasped.

"No one ever killed it yet," said Ruben. "Maybe we should try."

"What is it?" asked Paul, his curiosity piqued.

"No one ever saw it," Ruben said with certainty.

"Let's play!" said Betty, bouncing on her toes. "I'm the fortune teller. Right?"

"I'm king still!" Paul said, reminded of his reign.

"No one else is king," confirmed Ruben.

"No one else wants to be king but you," Betty grinned.

"Quiet, witch!" said Paul.

"I'm the fortune teller. There's no witch," Betty told Paul.

"Same difference! Fortune tellers are witches!" reasoned Paul. "Burn her!" he ordered, pointing his stick at her again.

"Your majesty," said Ruben, in a show of deference.

"Huuh?" Paul nearly stammered before he recouped a more haughty air, and said, "You say you're my right hand?"

"Yes, your majesty. I'm at your service," said Ruben.

"Then I command you to execute this witch by beheading on the guillotine," Paul roared.

"As your right hand man," Ruben started, "may I offer you my wise counsel?"

Paul studied Ruben with one eyebrow raised. "Sure, go ahead," he said. "That's what a right hand man's for."

"First of all, good king Paul," Ruben started, "It's better to burn witches. Decapitation doesn't always work."

"*RU*-ben!" Betty scolded him. "I thought you were on my side!"

"Burn her!" hooted Paul, triumphant. "Burn the stinkin' witch!" This last order so tickled him he was reduced to an episodic giggle fit.

"Secondly," continued Ruben, raising his voice for the first time of the afternoon and repeating,

"Secondly, even though witches are fortune tellers, fortune tellers are not always witches."

"She is!" argued Paul. "BURN the bedbug!"

Her attention fixed on Ruben, Betty chided Paul for interrupting, "Be quiet!"

"How dare you speak to your king that way!" raged Paul. "My right hand will punish you for your impotence!" He consulted Paul, "Whaddayou recommend?"

Keen to play, Ruben quashed a yen to correct Paul's vocabulary. "Since she's a fortune teller and not a witch, and since the actual witch knows the secret identity of the monster and how to defeat it so that the spell is broken and your people are freed, we should find out from the fortune teller where the witch is hiding."

"Where's the witch, Bedbug?!" demanded Paul.

"What's wrong with you?" Betty begged. "Since when was king another word for shithead?"

"I'll kill you myself, Betty Maguire, Bedbug and Liar!" threatened Paul.

"A king," exclaimed Ruben quickly to draw Paul's attention, "never dirties his hands. Especially not when they need someone's help."

"She called me a shithead!"

"Well, you are kinda being pretty shitty to her," Ruben said.

"Yeah, ya stupid shithead!" Betty stuck her tongue out at Paul. "Come on, Betty," Ruben reasoned, "you're trying to annoy him, which is not helping."

"He's annoying ay eff!" insisted Betty.

"You invented annoying from your mom's poop!" Paul countered. Whatever response he expected, his jibe sparked Betty to squeal with laughter while Ruben eyed Paul silently for a very long moment, his neck and shoulders drawn back. Paul tried for a second to feel laughed at, but when Betty repeated the words with some difficulty due to her continued shrieking, he caved in and cracked up with her.

Ruben finally smiled but held onto his need to police his playmates on several levels. When the chortles died down, he was the first to speak. "So, we're still playing Kingdom. Right?"

No longer standing, Paul sat on the fallen trunk close to Betty, his branch in hand. "I'm king, Betty's a fortune teller, and you're my trusty right hand," he recited like a babe never schooled in dispute. "What's the plan, brother man? Are we gonna waste this monster, or what?"

"I say we ask the fortune teller if she can tell us where to find it, your majesty," said Ruben, resuming his part as the king's man.

Without standing or waving his pretend sword, Paul managed to say to Betty what he said next: "Tell us, Madame Fortune Teller, where can we find the secret monster?"

"And," Ruben piped in, "Will we be able to defeat the thing to free the people?"

"Yeah! And also," chimed in Paul with his energy back on the upswing, "Does Excelsior have enough magic to kill it or do we need something else?"

"I understand the questions," declared Betty in a monotone that revealed she was serious. "Everybody close your eyes while I ask the leaves to give us the answer."

"Okay," said Paul, "my eyes are closed."

Ruben sighed deeply and said, "Okay-y, mine too."

The boys were silent while they listened to the crinkling of dry leaves as Betty scooped handfuls up from the ground and crumpled them in her fingers. "Holy spirits of the old crunchy leaves that cover the woods from here to the end of the world, tell me what you know about the secret monster that's keeping the kingdom under its evil curse." Then she scooped up more leaves and crushed then, singing an improvised chant as she did so, "Ooohh waa eee. Ooohh waa ooo. Leaves fall down. Trees all grow. Ooo wahh wee. Wooo waa oh. Tell me everything you know!"

"Whoa," whispered Paul, his eyelids squeezed tight. "That was cool."

"Sshhhh!" Betty shushed him sharply. "The leaves are talking!"

"What'd they say?" Paul could scarcely contain his excitement.

"Follow me," Betty said.

The boys opened their eyes and did as Betty told them, with Ruben in the lead until Paul pulled rank, offering a plausible reason. "I'll stay behind her so you can make sure we don't get attacked from behind by minions."

"You can never trust those minions," Ruben agreed.

The trio started off, following a path they had come to call just that, "The Path." It snaked along through the woods that remained behind the newish homes built over the past decade in their neighborhood, Meadowbrook Farms. The old farm was long gone. The trees that most local people believed were part of an old, recently-cut forest, actually grew up in pastures surrendered to a generation of more or less natural growth. Adults very rarely ventured here — out back — and because of this absence, the scale of the trees felt welcoming to small, young people. Here was a vast and diverse terrain of vividly changing worlds for these and other kids living in homes on the streets bounding it: a tropical jungle, a haven for the fey folk, Indian territory (Chautauqua or Calcutta), an uncharted planet in deepest outer space, a realm at the bottom of the ocean, a kingdom under the deadly curse of a monster no one has ever seen.

As it was still early spring, only a very few insects darted past, raising more curiosity than irritation. One tree in particular was adorned with such an abundance of inchworms twisting on barely visible threads that they were startled, then delighted. Paul's glee was so great that he fell into character. "It's a trap!" he declared and began to swing his stick this way and that. "The monster must have sent these poisonous inchworms to stop us! Aarrr!! HYAAHH!!!" he snarled and made quick work of the larvae's fine threads.

Betty and Ruben stood back at a safe distance while Paul enjoyed his frenetic defensive tactics. Once he had dispatched the inchworms, he took a wild swipe at the tree, slightly cracking his weapon. "Whuu-ut!?" he huffed, galled and looking from the trunk to his stick to his companions and back. "Is it...?" Paul examined the crack closely. Then, he told the others, "It's not broken. Okay? It's still invincible," he explained.

"Wait!" Betty suddenly commanded, her hand held aloft like she wanted a classroom teacher to call on her. She knelt down slowly to turn over a leaf with her other hand. "This leaf still holds the thoughts of someone powerful who went past here a little while ago."

"WHO?!" Paul grilled her, "What'd they — who was it?"

"The witch!" Betty said after listening a moment to the leaf.

The birds and squirrels chirped and chittered that the trio loitered thereabouts.

"The birds are making a lotta noise," noticed Ruben, lifting his head to search the arbors around them.

"What does that mean?" Paul looked eagerly from Ruben to Betty. "Is the witch close?"

Betty answered, rapid and sure, "No. I know where the witch is hiding."

"Where?" Paul held his breath.

"This way," Betty led them along a nearby shortcut towards a spur on the path.

Paul lagged a moment and Ruben passed by him, then stopped. "Coming?" Ruben asked.

"Where we going?" Paul wanted to know.

"To find the witch," directed Betty.

"Kill the monster. Save the kingdom. Remember?" Ruben bolstered.

"What's down this way?" asked a wary Paul.

"The witch," Betty replied artlessly.

"Isn't the quarry down here?" verified Paul.

"A ways from here," Ruben confirmed.

"My mom'll kill me if we go to the quarry," said Paul, unmoving.

"What? Are you gonna tell?" Betty taunted, repaying his earlier teasing.

"It's really dangerous, Betty!" insisted Paul.

"We're not even going that far!" Betty assured him. "That's not where the witch is at."

"How do you know there's even a witch, Betty Maguire?" challenged Paul.

"I'm a fortune teller," Betty boasted. "I can see things other people can't see."

"Unless you don't wanna be king anymore," said Ruben. "Betty can be queen then."

"I'm still king!" Paul asserted, gripping his branch firmly. "I just don't wanna get in trouble."

"Nobody's gonna get in trouble if nobody squeals," Betty reasoned firmly. "Now, let's go!"

"Alright," Paul caved. Then he perked up. "Watch out, you crazy witch! We're gonna get you and your stinkin' monster once and for all!"

"Long live king Paul!" cheered Ruben.

"Long live king Paul!" Betty chimed in.

The two of them chanted this at least a score of times in unison until they spotted a small cabin set back from the trail some thirty feet. Betty halted and motioned with her index finger in front of her puckered lips to be quiet. Then she pointed at the wooden structure and mouthed silently, "The witch is over there."

Paul froze as Betty moved towards the shack and Ruben pushed past him. "You guys," Paul half-pleaded.

Ruben and Betty turned and coaxed him. "We're here now," Ruben assured. "Might as well finish what we came to do."

They all looked at the derelict shelter with its lean-to roof and vertical boards weathered to a gray that revealed such age it seemed to hide a great stash of untold stories. And while Betty and Ruben could hardly resist this promise, heading on to discover more, Paul mistrusted their impulse to know what must be unknown for a reason. "What's in there??" he called after them, though neither had reached the door.

"That's what we wanna find out," Ruben explained.

"I'm pretty sure the witch lives there," said Betty.

"Well, tell her to come out here," Paul said.

"If we all go in together, we can corner her more easy," strategized Betty.

"Well," Paul started to reason, "since I'm king, you two scout ahead while I make sure we're not ambushed."

"If ya ask me, your highness," advised Ruben, "I think it's better for you to go in with us. Especially seeing as you have Excelsior and it's prob'ly the only thing that'll hurt the witch or the monster."

"Yeah," Betty confirmed, "besides, you don't wanna be caught out here by yourself. It'll be them two against one; meaning you're the one, and that would suck eggs."

"Well, okay," Paul capitulated. "But let's stay close then. Nobody split up. K?"

"I'll open the door," Betty said as she did so.

"You next," Ruben directed Paul. "I gotchou."

"We got this," Paul said, choking up on his Excelsior like a seasoned batter.

From outside, it appeared to be a one room shack not much bigger than an outhouse. Once through the door, the hut's narrow profile stretched back through a soot-smeared kitchen to an inner doorway that opened into a second room branching to the left. Through its shattered window, darkened and breached by a riotous tangle of brambles and briar branchlets and sprigs, no light or color entered so that the room's details — save for its cobwebs covered in dusty shadows — were obscured.

Betty must've rushed back to that rear space immediately as she detected it. Or so it seemed to Paul as he inched his way inside. He stopped and called out to her, causing Ruben to inadvertently flatten the back of Paul's sneaker, scraping his heel and further rattling the would-be king's nerve so that he dropped Excelsior to the patchy floor and made no move to retrieve it or adjust his pancaked shoe back.

Ruben plaintively huffed his name. "Stop blocking the door!" He shoved the resistant Paul slightly forward, enough to wedge his way inside just as there arose a great clatter from the hidden section of the next room, followed by a dull thud and a pronounced silence.

"Betty?" wheezed Paul, " — are you— ?"

A sharp shriek shut him up. Obviously, he'd forgotten he had any part in the game Betty and Ruben still determined to play to its climax.

Suddenly, Betty reappeared, laughing as if completely unglued and swinging what looked like the discolored remains of a furry creature over her head. Her mouth was twisted into a ghastly leer, purplish and bruised.

"Betty! Omigod!?!" said Ruben, excited by what he deemed a very creative improvisation on her part. "Is the witch in there?" he quizzed her.

"You fool!" Betty jeered, interrupting her fur flinging routine. "Your pathetic fortune teller is dead! I have possessed her soul! For I am the witch!" Then she launched into a string of maniacal howls.

"Your majesty!" Ruben commanded Paul. "Excelsior! Quick! It's our only hope!"

But Paul stayed rooted to his spot while Betty rushed forward, her lipstick-smeared face screeching as she did. "Neverrr!" Displaying an agility that filled both boys with polar extremes of awe, she swept up the branch and thrust it out through the small window over the cracked and grimy slop sink. She then resumed swirling the once pink, now rust-colored feather boa overhead. "I am victorious! And you are my slaves!"

This condition flicked a switch in Paul's inertia. With Betty leaning too close for comfort, he shot back, "I'll never be your slave! I'm king, you stupid witch! I am all powerful!!!"

Unexpectedly, Betty kissed him on the mouth and cackled with impish delight. "Now I've given you the kiss of death! Resist me and you will die, slave!"

Shocked to his core, Paul's reflex was to lash out, unhinged, with a wild punch landing on Betty's shoulder at the same time as he sneered in disgust and alarm.

"You hit me!" Betty thundered. "The spider saw you do it! I showed you mercy! SHE WILL NOT!!!"

"Shut the hell up, Bedbug!" Paul whirled around toward the door and was momentarily alarmed to find Ruben standing there, bemusedly. "Some right hand man you are, ya friggin' nerd!" He reached to push Ruben aside when — an instant before making contact — they both noticed the enormous black spider with yellow markings on its legs planted motionless on the back of his hand. Holding his arm aloft just so, Paul could only manage to unleash one very loud and very extended syllable from his mouth: "MAAAAAAAAA!!!"

Nebula, Anvil, Pillow, Head
(Eros & Psyche after the end of the world)

BOOK THE FIRST

the Ten Sefiroth refer either to the Ten Manifestations of God; the Ten powers or faculties of the Soul; or the Ten structural forces of Nature, the same quantity of Manual Digits. And let us not forget our Ten Hundred Year long ability to countenance a systemic punitive Decimation – the forfeiture of One Life in Ten from each of the Nine Known Native Nonconformist Cohorts whose nine hundred batches of living Lives Leftover flout Order in the avowal of a solemn purpose to 'defeat utterly' their tormentors (Accounting effected by Metrics we sequence in as many Ciphers — from base Zero to Nine) — i.e. Advocates, Adherents and Administrators of the Orthodox until the Whole is left to holding the rightly noisome – albeit tuneful – Ball of Confusion. Ten-Ten WINS, baby! Everybody ever grew up in the TriState know that. And besides!

All those last holders of Negro Birth certification spin their story full of sudden starts and stint.

no artists who attribute our parts on earth to mark re the O.G. orisha also do multi-dimensional multiverse as a matter of necessity. It takes three days for a lodger to bond to a house. And a house is an imperfect box for portraying its living infrastructure, for displays of its flesh and bone framework, for light shined on the tangled pulse of think and meat reinforcing every screw fast in each panel and board, for exposing stress where sinews and nerves charged with drawing out the constant orders to change the last blueprints of laughter and hurt that underpin the shelter it delivers as long as needed, for rounding out the shared ties its regular occupants enjoy. It is written: "la premere nuyt soit tenu pur estraunge... le autre nuyt geste..."1 [the first night one is taken for a stranger... another night, a guest...]; thereafter, this visitor becomes hoghenhine ("et la terce nuyt oune hyne."),[2] a household member who gains the legal right to abide with room and board; so fast holds this attachment that the Country Justice contends if this person "offend the Kings Peace, his Oast must be answerable for him."[3]

In this way, far from his native shores — a river's banks teeming with life that never ceases to take shape — Majigiza returns Blackwater to his only one and True Blue Bestie above all lesser and low Lay Folksies, Swee' Li'l Lee.

Through each morning, over noon, until evening wanes daylight, our fellow biped critters engage in labors made out of and into the common will to a safe and sanguine sanctuary for all and for one. Great tons of great masses carved sharp as flat whole notes from tendon and blood and synapse into songs to sing to the stirring of sand and water and aggregate for erecting solid state architectures shaped between wood planks held fast using screws and tape measures and dulled blades on saws in accord with dictates drawn up out of Pythagorean equations that square up — let's say — three and four and five as neatly as five and twelve and thirteen on the surface of a gas-bounded sphere that feels flat enough to set over a timeframe containing the magnetic gravity of electrons which combine with each other as snugly as the one beat in the upstroke of her roundly-fleshed brown-assed hips thrust forth to greet the downbeat of his hit-it-back hard and piston-grip – slinky, deep and dank skinshaft, lubricious and stinky, smack-dabbled slurpery in her queef squish a-pounding, as if no other two bodies any elsewheres under a moonless night sky all pointed at billions of outer space lights might locate the bright polka-dots peeking out from behind time untold that neither she nor he can see or hear, a past so perfect it cannot be spoken by this very storyteller with any semblance of truth, definitely not with any kind of respect (always, this tired, old nonsense and its insensitive demand for respect) for the where or wherefore.

And as is the common folly of such folk who fortify what they see for themselves against life eternal — free of form and dropped back of the reinforced concrete facade built upon what became a bulwark that could only pretend to stand for shelter, for one more monolith hardly impenetrable, twice flat-backed and square-faced, shouldering wings long gone rigid, gone useless, enormous cementitious-cast wings cut out to adorn and nothing more — people swallowed this fakery whole cloth and daily, dazed into dangerous denial of their own deity.

BOOK THE SECOND

Majigiza's ceaseless wanderings reverse and resume with the rhythm of rock and sledge. When these fucking lovers turned a-loose unto the next generation a real life bundle of boy who reached out from his unschooled childishness for twice the love these two surviving adults — now playing the respected role of parent one and parent two — both imagined they were told by the law on how to give love for all grown-ups (despite the powerful-acting childish contagion) to make them, two, also choose to love twice what man's mortal law forbids wanting (like waiting to weigh out measure for measure) to do (not unlike it wants you to feel now, seventeen or maybe twenty years before the story unfolds, in a past so identical to the one you now hold before you).

Breakfast is moot in nutrients and a hundred percent upchuck spewed out splotch about face right down to the kitsch looking kitchen floor tile.

Then came the break: a report from noose channel heaven covering clouded dead peoples who think they live again, saying, "In all serious be that as it is, and if i'm getting this correct, Lee, aka miss witchita 9000, help me out here, Shelter."

Of a demeanor Lee deems deliberately deceptive,

dead-on dark, downright discombobulating –
the anchor's away. "Folks," he hollers, "is this not
unsinkable, ya goddamn 5000 year old fucking queen
of the lake at the top of the goddamn old but sorely
fucked for forty four years wrinkly butt? I mean,
you are still you, ya regal, big-asseded, airy hay-hole
billowing sulfur and methane in clouds of invisible
but thick as thieves thought up by Thanatos during
a love affair you two both started three thousand
thousand times errors squared to last whole and
unsullied eons ago..." (and also, just as aghast, we
might add – as must we mighty ghost narrators of
our omniscient science still greater than gods will and
are want to do – including the seventh i am that i am
– his popped eye dangling on the very nerve of him
six feet long and ever under afoot, the one and a half-
eyed king as I speak; I, the most telling narrative spin
doctor of all free degrees at the outskirts of quantum
space in perpetual material science, I carry capacities
and content to dismay all listeners.

So riddled with this, the mystery viral, deep and
microbial, a most lethal cannonball lecturer and
avowed vegan delinquent, a sworn quixotic custodian
of a deliquescence delightful to billions – this ad
brought to you by the last american narrators' council
on greater distraction, from what you hear on, shouts
to the departmental security will remain unheard of
outside the compartment you are specifically pigeon-
holed in.

She tells it like this: Social Regulatory Reviews are
unfair.

Of course, She is beautiful, She is brown, She is
shapely like a proper hourglass perfectly regulates
grains flowing down until out.

She: Shelter.

She rhymes with Lee.

He adds: It's easy enough to clean up the
postpartum detritus – placenta, omphalos, feces,

coagulated blood, slimy viscous green gone gray, yelling purely yellowbellied sap, sucker. Slap one for deep breath, choking on mother cunt juice and hospital air.

The functionary concludes: We understand, which is why she will be placed under departmental custody until full compliance has been determined at a date as yet undetermined.

She pleads: What?! But when?

Which He reasons, squeezing his hand in her paws, tearing his flesh wound deeper: Not now, love. It's fine. I'll see Ra. His father and me are old friends.

She cries unconsolable: But, no! Majigiza, you blackguard, you freak! You've been flagged! And besides, the old birdbrained bastard is dead!

He ponders a profusion of possible come-ons, his priapus stiffer than his resolve until asking her: Which one?

She spit beyond belief, her whiskers twitching, her claws digging at the armrest and shredding its already tattered upholstery; she spits some more: Ksch-shshshschsshhh!

Both of them! What a crocodile of shit! The functionary suddenly slaps the question mark patched on the front of his conical cap, obscuring the pineal chakra even as he rises up from his seat lotus-legged in a jittery pose that one would think counter to the levitation he achieves nonetheless (as if free of exertion, or so it appears to the terrorized featherbrain osprey-headed godguy, the pussycat's paramour): You strike me as a couple whose ciphers post well above the mean. Why you failed to stick with the regimen mandated for postpartum corporeal estate per your age height and birth gender escapes me, baby.

Blackwater bristles, down on his neck all a-ruffle: N-ni-ni-ni – ¡!@#$%^!??!¡

The functionary curls his upper lip and cuts his eye at Lee, ignores Majigiza. "In legends and popular stories," he goes on, points at her: "a witch, Ol' Higue, you was getting ready to shed yer skin." The functionary explains himself to Blackwater, "... so she could fly off sometimes in the form of a ball of fire in search of sleeping people, especially to suck a baby's blood. You could know she was a obeah-lady by the red eyes, blazing. A blood-sucking Old Higue, too. Everything 'bout her had a dangerous ring to it."[4]

old hige? asks a wee, young babe leaving off suckling at its mother's teat.

old higue. the mother nods and, her clutched babe latched fast, a squinty eye open and peering curious and skeptical at Lee.

ole high, Shelter mocks the functionary, chuckling.

ole higue, frowns the functionary, firm, resolved, making a third syllable to augment the two.

ole ige. Blackwater growls, dropping the third syllable to underscore the functionary's bloody-minded buffoonery.

Ol Hige! Ol' Hige! Ol' hi-gue! chants the tot, benign, sing-song, and adds a third syllable the third time around for no real reason other than to fit his incantation.

old heg, the baby mama feels the need to teach the child something as they sit waiting in public, scrutinized by all and sundry in the hall (simply because folk are in the habit of inspecting babies and babies' mothers who enter public places at any time around the world).

ole heg, the functionary grins idiotically at the babe — all the more due to his apparent failure to taste the pool of black ink staining his fat bottom lip and — back of this lip — the row of little baby teeth steady blackening due to his having sucked and chewed so long and dutiful at the pen still blacking his blacked chompers backsides and frontsides.

ole haig, Lee mocks him again and shakes her head, scornful and dangerously incredulous —

worries Majigiza — given her place directly before the functionary who so obviously wears the stereotype of obedience and daft-headedness, the cliche-assed dullard (or dolt) of dastardly deeds done for neither money nor reward in a dystopia doomed to a dearth of both and more until someone (at least), — someone exactly repeatable develops them and therefore, at least — someone acts solely outside the rote banality of someone acting not evil, no good, no matter how much our chocolate-colored champions do not watch the cannot-be-missed Appointment at Nuremberg's black-slash-white beady wire gold-plated rimmed spectacles of the paradigm of the banal.

Finally, the functionary leaves his post and the lovers we know how I told you so — Majigiza and Lee, whose wild afro mane makes like a magnet for fingers trying to mane-handle her uninvited — get up and go. They levitate. The floor drops. The door swings out and offs the coat hooks the lovers leave behind windows the wind defenestrates.

BOOK THE THIRD

We don't need no jackets, he thinks. It's summer.

Yeah, but we headed for outer space, she thinks as a reminder.

Yeah, but technically, we there now. Outer space. You know?

Yeah, okay, Mistah TECH-nickel, she thinks.

Damn coat hooks ain't gettin' no-oo- o closer. We should eat, he thinks. That'll get us warm. Yeah, it will. Except I'm not hungry.

We can order take-out.

We still have to eat it right away. Can't bring no food out in the astral plane.

No wings on the astral plane? he grins, thoughtlessly.

You stupid! You got jokes! You nah corny, Monoceros, too late.

He gazes at the picture of perfection, of Shelter, of storms left out, and loves the feeling he feels himself filling up his feelings with.

She smiles and starts to give in to her own loving feelings. She thinks, you got that.

He looks down and extends far out into a collapsing kaleidoscope of dizziness.

In every Vertigo, Lee thinks, there's this condition of being overshadowed or darkened. Like a darkening or blacking-out. You don't know if it's by shade. You can't say if it's by gloom. You got the dense obtenebration with which the object you travel outside is surrounded — which could mean you're surrounded, joined[5] with a great big mothafuckin Semblance of Turning Round,[6] my nigga. He knows it too well and starts to think back, Can you see chiaroscuro under the Sun, Moon, Stars, and Light?[7] He slips and starts spinning around and around his root, his limbs akimbo and speedy, all slap-happy even though he is not, even in the breezy calm awash in the following thought: There's no reason why we should not apply the adjective 'unicursal' to denote those figures whose journeys consist of a single unbranched path.[8]

She loosens up and lets out a real gut-busting, barrelhouse howl.

He holds a coin dead center her high brown brow.

She looks through it and thinks aloud, With us, mothafucka — like alternatives — the pattern becomes 'multicursal.'[9] Like you sing the term as its complement, or as its opposite.[10]

Maze, thinks Majigiza, suggests to me a multicursal design... where confusion arises.[11]

[The reader's progress through these labyrinths of language thus forms a multicursal pattern.][12]

Shelter did not think otherwise, though compelled to opine, Why not think of the network as being made up of more complex diagrams and directional veers: multicursal mazes, connect-the-dots, cross-currents, winding pathways, concentric circles, pentagrams?[13]

Blackwater sees her tears splash her teeth, the sparkle triggers the thought that: One may serve as the type of a compact — and the opposite example, it might serve as that of a diffuse — not necessarily mirrored, in any case (leather, snakeskin, ostrich).

A meteor shower burns down from the sky, a sometimes bright, lighted up multicursal labyrinth.[14]

Lee's voice belies her thinking (or stops the narrator to confess)... I conclude that letters will occasionally come to heaven, and always be written in — the other place.[15]

Majigiza cannot break the centrifuge, or an orbit alternates in paradise or the other place while it happens that Lee is gracious to him, or indifferent.[16]

Shelter extends gratitude her way, she forgets to even give or take more, thanks to others. For example, she thinks, Shall I go to heaven for doing that? Or mayn't I rather go to the other place, mothafucka?[17]

He's nervous, too. He got jokes and frowns, or a radio guy says gut feeling feels real thought, real talk, more brains. Blackwater thinks, I wouldn't much care to go to heaven myself; all my friends are in the Other Place.[18]

Far below, fields of lush, green treetops, blue rivers, blacktops, gray rock, brown dirt patch roads all grow slow and steady smaller, furtherer faraway.

Lee feels something real in her gut, kind of like under her gut, back of her gut, kind of like backbone. So she wants the names and numbers of vertebrae, like which ones are scared,

sacred, and just how. She grabs Blackwater tight, thinks, There being neither youth or age, sir, in the 'eavenly mansions — no, nor in the other place either.[19]

Majigiza fields emotion you know against the rules and thinks back to her, Rousseau bade the panurgic one to attend to his own affairs.[20]

Shelter thinks quickly, No less panurgic and less encyclopedic a critic than Diderot himself[21] could argue for the compelling force of the environment.[22]

This radicalizing process in both their Constitutions gets accomplished finally under Lord Jim Jam, the Panurgic.[23]

The penultimate echelon, its astral plains, at last. Vast swaths full of currents empty right before the ruddy, bewitched lovers' eyes. From out of space all choking with swirling, stellar dusts emerges the issue of a febrile friction, its fervor, the frenzy that renews friendships, their blushing blooms.

Lee's eyes cloud with tears and familial sentiment as she thinks, Scarcely a decade ago most of us would have shuddered at the idea of a seven years' Bible study course adopted by most of the Protestant sects in common,[24] mothafucka. It's a program that makes the subjective[25] non-empiricist and idealist perhorresce uncontrollably.[26]

Blackwater takes her teasing in stride, and starts thinking, Our word 'superstition' has come to be used in a merely bad sense, and to mean a childish and craven religiosity. With the German word it is not so; therefore Goethe can say with propriety and truth: 'Aberglaube is the poetry of life.'[27] [To use a word Majigiza has almost naturalized, one rooted in a prior glaube,[28] a primary belief. The Scholar-Gipsy is a survival from an age when both Aberglaube and free thought flourished.[29] And finally, nostalgia for the Aberglaube of antiquity has impelled us to talk of reverence that salutes the sanctity of mutual love.[30]

Shelter wonders, Is that so? Without waiting for a reply she goes on to think, The censor censured; or,

The conscious lovers examin'd in dialogue between Marplot and Freeman. His employers on either[31] side should discard him as a mere Sir Martyn Marplot.[32]

Majigiza chuckles at length. He catches his breath and thinks, What Tippy! I'm a bit of a Marplot here...

Lee nods and thinks, This comes of entrusting your friends by halves.[33]

What a mothafuckin' marplot anxiety is![34] thinks Blackwater, as he slips his careful hand through her breast to caress her heart with a gentle warmth she quietly welcomes.

Lee slowly comes to a stop and he, too, floats to rest at her underside, assuming the brunt of the eddies' charged flux with his bulk.

Shelter thinks, But what is the use of my taking the vows and settling everything as it should be, if that marplot mothafucka Hans comes and upsets it all?[35]

Conscious that Hans haunts a distant nebula far beyond further consideration, Majigiza massages Lee's uterus. She runs her fingers through his knuckles and they listen to their diploid's gametes couple to discover and catalog their own common experience.

Papi thinks, In future campaigns the lieges shall not be; no more of the mothafuckin' marplots they were in the heady days of Lord Raglan.[36] Fate: the marplot,[37] mothafuckas.

Mami relaxes damn near completely or lets herself melt through Papi's every pore until they mimic the little gametes, still unseen. She thinks, Colonel Nicholas was a meddler and a marplot with a genius for intrigue,[38] a true blue follower in the footsteps of such marplots, Marxists, Maoists or malignants as the Lords Robbins and Bridges.[39]

Blackwater grins in agreement. The three of them must relinquish the euphoria of this unitary aesthetic or blindly bear it through each and every condition; put it to rights — spoken, secret, an order no things determine or undermine. Like we feel squeezed in shells we arm with the radii and arrhythma-thematic mind to test as many material possibilities as we may observe together.

This is what Blackwater thinks, Politicians teamed with veteran marplot Jesse Helms of North Carolina to filibuster the theory to death's door.[40]

Lee loves his shell and opens up into the extra inches as she thinks, As if that spoils or defeats a plot or hinders an undertaking, mothafucka.

He casts a scowling glance imagining the incorrigible man[41] he knows does not fit with them. Majigiza thinks, There were some of his fellow-countrymen populist pimps whose marplot disclosures seemed likely to bring down a new onslaught of hungry, huddled masses.[42]

Shelter sighs through their doubled lungs and adds the thought, Beyond the tender mercies of meddling, mothafuckin' marplot fortune.[43]

Blackwater glides. Enveloped, sanguine within, Lee rides, their zygote with them. He would swear his common oath: Be Lethen and be Flegeton.[44]

She cries aloud and his throat opens wide before her muscular tongue, exhales a zephyr that fans not only their ardor, but a river of fire, To Achæron, & Phlegethon: dare you venture to do it?[45]

His laughter trebles with the levity of her amity. The inner child who swamps their organs listens, hears Blackwater.

The oath continues, once reared, unstoppable, The hell of waters! where... the sweat Of their great agony, wrung out from this, Their Phlegethon, curls round the rocks of jet That gird the gulf around.[46]

Looking down from this pinnacle upon the howling, flaming licks spit out of the boiling river Phlegethon below, One could not help smiling.[47] No phlegethon could be found that would burn them.[48] But slip a foot on frost-spiked stone Above this rocklipped Phlegethon And you shall have The Black Rock of Kiltearn For tombstone.[49] And now their unborn child unravels a nourishing thought it cannot think for long or aspire to breathe this day: In the bed of Ingratitude flows — with rapid flood — the Phlegethon of oblivion.[50]

Notes

1 Britton, F. M. Nichols (1865) I. 49 (MED), c1290.

2 Britton, F. M. Nichols (1865) I. 49 (MED), c1290.

3 Countrey Justice, M. Dalton (rev. ed.) xl. 98, 1630.

4 Spice, O. Kempadoo Buxton (1999) 84, 1998.

5 History of Salt, E. M. Boddy, ii. 25, 1881.

6 Sylua Syluarum, Bacon, §725, 1626.

7 Court of Gentiles: Pt. I, T. Gale (ed. 2) iii. x. 99, 1672.

8 Mazes & Labyrinths, W. H. Matthews. xxi. 184, 1922.

9 W. F. J. Knight Cumaean Gates iv. 60, 1936.

10 Mazes & Labyrinths, W. H. Matthews. xxi. 185, 1922.

11 Mazes & Labyrinths of the World, J. Bord, i. 9. 1976.

12 Labyrinths of Language, W. B. Faris, iv. 86, 1988.

13 Clicking, F. Popcorn & L. Marigold, ii. 217, 1996.

14 Mazes & Labyrinths, W. H. Matthews, xxi. 185, 1922.

15 Letters 29 Dec. 1841in Record of Later Life (1882), , F. A. Kemble, II. 156.

16 Gilded Age, 'M. Twain' & C. D. Warner, xi. 108, 1874.

17 Duke's Children, Trollope, I. xx. 245, 1880.

18 Penny Plain, 'O. Douglas' i. 13, 1920.

19 Open House, 'M. Innes' xi. 101, 1972.

20 Rousseau I, J. Morley. 291, 1873.

21 Diderot II, J. Morley, xvii. 279, 1878.

22 Science, 869/1, 8 June 1906.

23 Silent Years, J. F. Byrne, x. 105, 1953.

24 Princeton Review, Jan. 31, 1882.

25 Journal of Philosophy, Psychology & Scientific Methods 2 396, 1905.

26 Fortn. Rev. Apr. 544, 1895.

27 Literature & Dogma, Matthew Arnold, 77, 1873.

28 Contemporary Review, Oct. 1873, p. 794.

29 PMLA, 1962, 77 295/1

30 Leigh Hunt & the Poetry of Fancy, R. S. Edgecombe, iii. 103, 1994.

31 R. Steele (title), 1723.

32 Vindic. Brit. Colonies, J. Otis 21, 1765.

33 Town before You, H. Cowley, v. 87, 1795.

34 Letters of Countess Granville. May (1894) I. 295, 1824.

35 Daniel Deronda, 'G. Eliot.' II. iv. xxxii. 321, 1876.

36 Invasion of Crimea, A. W. Kinglake (ed. 4), VI. ix. 380, 1880.

37 Fate the Marplot, F. T. Woodington, 1915.

38 American History Review, no. 45, p. 343, 1940.

39 The Economist (Nexis), 25 Nov. 123, 1978.

40 Time (Nexis,) 27 Dec. 12, 1982.

41 The Lancet, 10 Apr. 64/1, 1824.

42 Invasion of Crimea, A. W. Kinglake, VI. ix. 230. 1850 (1877 ed.).

43 Vashti, A. J. Evans, xxviii. 392. 1869.

44 Confessio Amantis (Fairf.), Gower, v. 1109. 1393.

45 Bugbears, J. Jefferes, iii. iii. 119. c1564 (1911).

46 Childe Harold: Canto IV, Byron, lxix., 37. 1818.

47 "Descent into the Maelström," in Tales, by Edgar Allen Poe, p. 87. 1845.

48 "Behaviour." in The Conduct of Life, Ralph Waldo Emerson, p. 170 (U.K. ed.). 1860.

49 "The Black Rock of Kiltearn," in Selected Poems, by A. Young, p. 42. 1935, reprinted 1998.

50 The Island of the Day Before, Umberto Eco, William Weaver tr., p. 377. 1995.

a shroud of unbearable silence veils the primeval sound that none can utter. the line that man and woman have drawn to separate earth from sky calls the searcher to cross a horizon his quest may never reach.

as iron rails are fixed to wood embedded in stone along a curve that hugs close to the flow of great waters, he wanders a wasteland of bankrupt industries whose ruins of manufactured stone and metals housed the plunder of vast woods cut clear, hard mountains reduced to mounds, their spirits mutilated by a thousand thousand thousand names whose meanings all spell fear.

he calls himself an artist although suspicious of what prods his senses to tell him he lives alone.

passing through an unguarded breach, he lets his guarded steps lead him to a trove of abandoned constructions that echo with the weeping of women wed to carpenters and lumberjacks, a lamentation oblivious to the distant laughter of trees whose return march across forgotten farms and emptied hamlets surrounds the urban hives of humans with a density that increases from one season to a next.

he calls himself an artist even as he calls the voice that resonates this peaceful tomb of recomposition his own, denies the knowledge that corrects his error as nothing before his love of creation. his knowing aside, his eyes and hands presume to control what he names a random selection process toward a production series that holds curiosity as its certain contingency, one that rattles discovery with uneasiness. his only rite is no different from ours, a repetition that struggles to straighten lines out of circles, cyclical rhythms that emboss the skins of maggots and brains as perfectly as every ouroboros and swallowtail.

does he hear what his muscle and nerve refashion from all this manufactured detritus?

does the earth shudder between its primordial roots in anticipation of a solar-kissed seed's growth through an axis that reaches from winter to summer, an ascent returned to the downstroke before it, a turn of tools given to lever and balance extending like blood baptized in each of the four chambers?

is his name what he needs to wear a crown affirming his fitness for a sacrifice without meaning?

does this drummer demand these words to enlighten what sound arrangements accompanied its unwritten mantra across oceans of timeless eternity?

on saturn and jupiter, on venus and pluto, on mercury's mission to deliver from mars a message invisible but under the light of the moon's robe of darkness!

on madison avenue breaking the news of wall street!

on paper spilled inky with lines in every direction that describe the infinity of spheres assembled as a history of being freed of all need because it is already free!

on ecstasy thundered up word and act between shadows that dance after heaven's indomitable light! this shape and that give nothing to everything that rides the horse of human encounters our drummers have beaten on like the ketzak of monkeys echoed in the gangan poetics of ayangalu.

may humanity invoke its assemblies of gods to restore this gesture to the quantum light we can only transform in service of all we have chosen to listen to and repeat after, to observe and to serve, to compose and decompose in joyful imitation of imagination restored to creation.

willy knew the fists hammering at his door belonged to the bonobo chimp pedro and ali the kodiak bear. this knowledge didn't make him feel especially happy feels. but he did know them well enough to open up as quickly as possible. delaying the inevitable would only invite calamity.

behind him, groggy and wearing only the flannel shirt willy had tossed aside when bedtime turned into playtime maybe an hour earlier, rasharanda complained, "it's fucking nearly four fucking o'clock in the fucking morning!"

"it's ali and pedro," willy explained. a reformed reprobate, he once thrived in cahoots with the notorious furman brothers. of the dozen or so loosely bound conspirators who once marauded under that name, the pair of hirsute henchmen right outside were the last hangers-on to their criminal fraternity of carnage and crazy.

rasharanda sighed in resignation. she had come to accept willy's will to hold space for comrades from the dark years. whether this suggested real charity to willy's credit or spelled rank indulgence made no difference. rasharanda agreed that the best way to restore this old cohort lay along a road repaved in acts of trust.

ali, the kodiak bear, rushed in wearing nothing but a necktie and a porkpie hat tilted at a rakish angle, a mailbag slung over his shoulder. the monkey sported a white cotton loincloth one could easily mistake for a diaper. "lock the door!" growled ali sharply.

willy peered quizzically at the bundle. ali set it on the floor. he eyed it like a cat waiting for a cornered mouse to make a last desperate bid for life. "uhh, is there somethin alive in there?" willy worried.

rasharanda, incredulous, also squinted at the squirmy suspect sack. "there's definitely some kinda sentient entity in there... and it wants out."

"get over here," ali grumbled to pedro. he pointed at the floor near the duffel. pedro bounded eagerly in place and squatted there, his haunches coiled.

ali took hold of the drawstring with one paw and secured the bag's mouth with the other. "on three," he warned pedro before starting the count. the prize inside the bag went still. "...three!" roared ali. and at that, he raised the package aloft topsy turvy and shook out a leprechaun.

"OMIGOD!!!" keened rasharanda as if hailing the dead, "WHAT THE ACTUAL FUCKING FUK?!?"

willy's jaw dropped. "a fucking leprechaun?!"

the leprechaun sat comfortably on his ample bottom. regaining his bearings, leveled the green bowler hat on his crown and set its bright red ibis feather erect. "aye!" he spoke up. "Laoise Caragh Omin Rajut Traik Poloi at your service, but you can call me Tod." his grin traced a vexatious curl between the crinkly crow's feet cornering his twinkly eyes as it ran under his fluffy nose behind a shaggy white beard.

"this can't be good," gasped rasharanda. "this isn't good."

it was well after midnight in the middle of june and the moon was so full that the steady and rapturous songs of various birds wafted along the crisscrossed airs out of the fields and deep woods surrounding the hilltop cabin to replace what no one said then.

"the young lady has a premonition," grinned the leprechaun. "can anyone put her at ease? comfort her maybe?"

"i don't know if it'll be easy, but i'd be happy to get

comfy with rasharanda anytime!” volunteered pedro, rubbing his palms together.

“pedro!” rumbled ali. the monkey instinctively snatched the leprechaun’s wrist and fixed his mug on the captive with the bullying look of one who bullies because bullied.

“so, uhhmmm,” willy struggled to clear his throat but it felt dried up and his words came out crackled and weak. “you guys kidnapped a leprechaun…?”

“we sure as shit did!” pedro proudly confirmed.

“which means he’s gonna tell us where his pot o’ fuckin’ gold is at!” spelled out an impatient ali. “ain’t that right, little man?”

“the rules,” started the leprechaun, “and there are always rules one must abide.”

“hogwash!” protested pedro. “rules is made for breakin’ i always say. and i ain’t the first.”

“i didn’t make em,” continued tod. “i’ve simply learned to follow them more or less after a few thousand years of not always pleasant but instructive lessons.”

“that’s a lotta hooey!” argued ali, rearing up. “everybody knows you fairy people is expert at flauntin various and sundry laws of god and man, not to mention nature and goddess and whatnot.”

“aye!” concurred tod. “but even for us, there’s a price. for example, the law of the forgotten land says that i’m never to be taken hostage under any circumstance. revealing the location of hidden booty is barely the tip of the atonement that faces me now.”

“atonement?” scoffed the monkey. “that ain’t nuthin but forgivin’ yourself and assumin’ the composure of metta and trust. guys like me do that all day. no biggee.”

“but wait a minute,” rasharanda piped in, her brown face still bloodless and taut. “aren’t you just talking about chasing rainbows? i mean, this pot o gold stuff is just a metaphor for the metta and trust you're talking about. right? kinda like the alchemical work n shit."

"by jim, i think she's onto something there, boys!" shouted the leprechaun.

"baloney!" ali blurted. "in the culture of late capitalism that seduces everyone to perform a role in the spectacle of production and consumption, a pot o gold is only metaphorical in da same way that money stands in for a future role that will replace the discomfort of the current one. as if inner calm comes of self-worth as a sign of belonging. me? i ain't felt like i belong to anythin in forever! that's why i'ma get me that booty so i can get me some belongings."

"listen buddy," pedro chimed in, "i never felt worthy of belongin to nothin neither. but bein pals witchu all these years is like a friggin godsend."

"i dunno," willy glowered as if to himself or no one, "this feels pretty ominous to me right now. i guess it's a good thing i don't believe in omens."

"aye," recognized tod, "as if omens are less worthy of belief than anything else. what do ya believe in then?"

"maybe i realize that my errors never really happened so i don't have to believe in things. especially things i don't understand."

"or maybe you understand things and got stuck standing under em," observed rasharanda.

"whatever's hidden ain't gonna correct nothin," warned ali. "that's why this midget's gonna unearth his booty."

"you speak of the hidden as if it's unknown," grinned the leprechaun, "but to know that it's hidden, you must know it already."

"but to know something doesn't mean you have it. right?" wondered rasharanda.

"does anyone have anything?" volleyed tod.

"maybe all that we have only proves we been had."

"yeah, yeah, yeah!" chattered pedro, impatient. "nobody knows love like love knows us. so what? right? i still want that gold."

just then, the fly on the wall who had been quietly sleeping until all the commotion startled him with a start that sent him flying straight into a spiderweb in the corner where wall and ceiling meet hollered at the group, "you motherfuckers got my ass stuck in this sticky stuff and made me this hungry bitch's next meal!" a thousand tears sprang from as many eyes and a cold nervous sweat rolled off his back.

"stop sweatin and strugglin, bub!" nagged the spider. "i'll suck your insides out later. i ain't hungry now."

"what the actual heck?" puzzled pedro. "as if there ain't no end to the mystery o life n death!"

"alright, enough o this mystery bullshit!" snarled ali. he bent down to stick his snout in front of tod's grill and scowled. "the gold, tiny critter! where is it? ante up!"

tod didn't flinch an inch. "cool your jets, big guy. i stash my keep in the kingdom of not."

"is that some kinda forgotten land?" asked rasharanda. "i never heard of it."

"she's a cartographer," willy explained.

"luckily, we don't need a map," tod smirked. "if me memory serves, there's an entrance right out back."

"how would you know?" challenged willy. "you been here before?"

"where haven't i been?" answered tod, winking as if the first wink. "we can out by the deck." he stood up to brush off the seat of the pants and started through the kitchen for the sitting room.

"maybe he has been here," mused rasharanda, watching the captive in awe.

"hold on a second there, mister thumb!" pedro sprang after tod and snatched hold of his arm. "no funny business."

that's when the spider yelled at the fly. "i told ya to stop all that wriggling! i been tryna digest this here caterpillar's guts all day but it ain't been easy. tastes like they was laced with roundup. not that it'll stop me from inhaling what you got if ya don't chill out!"

"help meeeeee!" the quintet heard the endangered pollinator squeal as they traversed the deck past the kitchen to the yard.

tod led his captors and their friends across the light spilling down from the moon to an old door that lay flat on the ground by the toolshed. "here we are," he sang. a mourning dove's cry answered him from the distance.

"and how da heck is dat?" pedro wondered. "i ain't seed rainbow da first."

"ya!" agreed ali. "and no hawthorne bush neither!"

"the whip-poor-will's warning!" guessed willy. "somebody's gonna lose their soul."

"that's a paloma," rasharanda corrected him. "the whip-poor-will's song is brighter. but it's a common mistake."

"i thought you didn't believe in omens," chuckled ali.

"that's not an omen," argued willy. "that's lore."

"so what's the story behind an old door laying on the ground?" chortled pedro.

"he was supposed to use it to replace the front door like five years ago," rasharanda remarked, rolling her eyes. "talk about ancient lore."

"well, since he never did so i suppose he wasn't supposed to," tod quipped. and then he fixed his attention on the door and ordained, "open up!"

with that, the unhinged door swung wide as if

on hinges and they heard the totally terrified and heart stopping screams of horror that arose out of all the little critters that had grown used to dwelling there undetected — scores of translucent grubs and spiders and earwigs and ticks and termites and larvae and worms and ants and their aphids (exactly who enslaved who is unclear) — so that our heroes covered their ears against the chorus of pains reverberating up from the scurry and scatter that displayed a sudden and awful purpose in the midst of lives that had long felt little if any need to ponder purpose. now: to evade the menace of moonlight reflecting a daylight that should have never revealed much more than its heavy lidded shadow through the distant cracks marking the door's perimeter.

"jesus fucking christ!" bellowed pedro. "i fukn love these lil beasties!" he teetered deftly on toes and fingers to scoop up hands full of startled bugs and things he shoveled into his gullet.

"i fukn hate em!" thundered ali as he jumped into the rectangle of light deprived grasses and roots and mycelium and soil and things to stomp them out. an instant later the ground beneath him dropped away and he plummeted from sight, howling perplexedly. then they heard a dull thud followed after a brief pause by the low sound of ali's "OWWIEEEEE!"

tod quickly jumped into the perfectly rectangular hole before anyone could exclaim "holy shit!" or "what the fuck?" even though willy and rasharanda both took the time to say so, respectively.

"well," mused pedro, "last one down's a human's uncle!" and down he leapt.

"this way," directed tod once everyone was assembled in the vast and vaulted chamber of root and stone teeming with mice and voles and slugs and salamanders and earwigs and countless critters like that all tending the young and old and occasionally knocking each other off when food more meaty than microbial fare was wanted. they turned the corner after tod and stumbled on an orgy of fucking bunnies too involved to care.

"hey!" pedro pointed at a long-legged female in the throes of her shorter partner's penetrating prowess. "i used to hang out with her when she said she'll never fuck again. now she's fukn her brains out!"

"rabbit brains are a sunset land delicacy at imbolc," smiled tod with fond recall.

"she musta lost her mind," pedro complained.

"we have no minds to lose," willy reproved him. "the one mind has us."

"for fuk's sake!" protested ali. "don't you ever get tired of smarty pantsing the hell outta life? how do ya stand it, randa?"

"it may be impractical, but it's all the same as everything else," pointed out rasharanda. "only different."

"ugh!" grunted ali, dismissive. "how far we gotta go?" he badgered tod.

"when we see red dragon, we're there," tod told him. "she's not far. i can smell her."

sure enough, as they rounded a hillock where the ground overhead hung uncomfortably low, they came upon a great crimson newt. "i'm red dragon," she announced. "you're here for tod's gold. are ya's?"

"that's right!" woofed ali, puffing out his sunken chest.

"technically," parlayed rasharanda, "me and willy only came along for the adventure."

"that's right," willy figured in. "my anarchist ass hates gold and all material obsessions."

"hatred of things merely masks an addiction to the false love of higher illusions," spat red dragon. and suddenly, she vomited out a very oblong and hot fountain of flame that roasted our characters' meat to medium rare. all except for tod.

a fox chomped on a blind vole. a opossum shuffled after a clutch of ticks with her nine babies hanging on for dear life. a skunk skittered after a couple of earthworms under the base of an oyster mushroom it also devoured. the mycelium linking beech to oak to maple to hemlock to the soil that links gravity to earth basked in the full underground light of a moon basking amidst implausible orbits the similarly solar infused spores careen between to unpack the vacuum of interstellar crossroads that never begin to go nowhere nobody can ever name.

"what's this about?" hooted a befuddled spirit hanging over the charred corpse that used to be ali. "i friggin love gold!"

"same difference," muttered red dragon sleepily.

"i feel all sparkly," confessed the ether around the burnt crisp formerly known as rasharanda.

"somethin tells me we the gold now," suspected pedro's cloudy residue as it wafted away from the smoldering cadaver that recently carried a name for rocks.

"i don't feel like me or anything at all even," willy cheered excitedly.

"it is kinda ecstatic," echoed the thought that escaped what used to be ali.

"this is really nothing happening," rasharanda's echo vibrated. "isn't that a song called heaven by talking heads?"

"if i wasn't sayin so myself," imagined that which never was ali, "i'd say we is love which is more than gold will ever be."

"we died! that's what tod means!" a voice attempted to utter.

"i don't mean anything!" tod said, curling up in the swirl of red dragon's tail.

"i love this," no one said.

"kewl," nobody breathed.

rasharanda woke with a start and nudged willy. he grumbled as she mused aloud, "i just dreamed the weirdest dream."

"this is the dream," willy scoffed. "that was real."

"anyways," she began and then told him everything she remembered of the dream that didn't happen the way she told it, if at all, like every other story we try to tell us.

Writer
[from The Book of Imaginary Human Beings
(with apologies to J-L.B.)]

"If I read this sentence, this story, or this word with pleasure, it is because they were written in pleasure..." writes Roland Barthes in his semiotic tract, The Pleasure of the Text. As for the built-in pleasure of words in print, that collaborative compilation long doing business as The Oxford English Dictionary numbers its entries at well over 600,000—each, chock full of meanings and citations from a virtual pantheon of pencil pushers—and all from twenty-six, purportedly meaningless ciphers. Of course, as Barthes might attest, were he not dead, English is hardly the only idiom in which writers write, and that which is and has been and will be written hardly approaches the sum total of all that must be told.

Who is this silent, solo scribbler? See him in the café window, sunlight dancing on his face as he tip tap taps at his portable, scritch scratch sketching imaginary roads that open up before the imagined feet of unimaginable beings in his rumpled notebook. See her study's sturdy escritorium support each inspired edit, writing all pretended wrongs as they never really happened. Word, phrase, sentence, paragraph, chapter, book, and verse; every one a temporary fix to a problem invented where no greater problem exists than the invention of problems that are not.

"That a thing should be written down is the first sign of its decay," cites Titus Burkhardt of one ancient, unnamable alchemist's spellbound book in some unnamed place not yet utopia long ago. Still longer ago, the ancient Egyptians rejoiced should their sons elect to be named scribes, for they would "do nothing" and still be paid in gold what most folks only hoped to dig in spades.

Closer to our time (according to writings ascribed to Plato), Socrates—who, like Jesus and the Buddha, never wrote (for, as St. Aquinas has written, the sound of the voice imprints upon the soul)—orated to his tyro, Phaedra, that in a universe where all things speak with one voice, a strictly peculiar persona devotes its "time to twisting words this way and that, pasting them together and pulling them apart, [and] so may fairly be called a poet or a speech-writer or a maker of laws." But this, maintained the ill-fated teacher, describes no philosopher, no lover of wisdom at all.

Imagine this as you birth another pretty paragraph of written labor: Fairy tale, tall tale, tattle tales, cock-and-bull story; each one, a childish variant on the dubious work of history, her story, my story, yours. Every word pronounced in every language round the world by every face that ever opened its fat cakehole is just another part of an impossible narrative still unfolding. Embodied in the human voice, living speech carries through our airspace on invisible waves, vibrations arising within the kinetic body focus in the throat and trigger correspondent sensations at the listener's ear. Simultaneously, the light emanating from the surfaces of objects—of people and things— flows over our retinas, stimulating an electromagnetic reciprocity. Entwined minds embellish the pictures painted over our eyes and ears, command a perpetual deep focus from horizon to periphery, blind to borders mapped out on economic orders, curious about what lies just beyond that point as far as the eye can see: a vista delimited by no paltry piece of paper.

Of a thin volume penned in French by Raoul Vaneigem, Belgian author of international situationist rambles and rants, poet laureate of the Lower East Side John Farris grumbled one winter morning, "Everything in this book is true; but impossible." Thus, proposed the aforementioned psychogeographer and flaneur, "It is not a matter of placing poetry in the service of revolution, but one of placing revolution in the service of poetry." And so, determined to spell it out for you—and for my Self—I wax poetic.

The Greatest Story Ever Told defies all space and time and may scarcely be proscribed by ink and press. Yet, legions of inky instigators cannot mind their p's and q's, fob their well-honed ink swill off as genius, plot dots and I's between what begins in order to resemble the end. Who is this egotist, this author, wedded to the wearisome wind that works so hard to lift his especially wizened wit up from the page? Historian, scientist, lawyer, poet: all writing is a fiction, an abomination that purports to render supra abundant energy into "proper" form. Does this orthographer imagine that this pleasure alone is an act of the Creative? Can this composer coerce the chaos he creates via his cause for control? Will this busy spelling bee ever cop to the poetry in motion, in stillness, the silence in sound? Abracadabra: An angel passes...

Bohemian champion Steve Cannon branded Darius James's caustic Negrophobia, "a curse." Bill Burroughs said, "writing is plagiarism" and, "language is a virus." Witch? Criminal? Or pest? It's a rotten business this penned man's ship squanders his pointy fingers on: seeking payback and approbation to indulge the first and blackest spell that your economy ever cast on our ecology; a dystopian world beginning with a misnomer—The Word—out of this old babe's mouth and malnourished without stint via an ungodly Naming of Things. Marshall McLuhan has responded to the lame threat aimed at our old friends—letters—by the burgeoning network of mechanized electric mediation by committing to the page this apt surmise: "...perhaps, as I've tried to demonstrate in my examination of the post-literate culture, the story begins only when the book closes."

ALSO OUT ON FAR WEST

farwestpress.com

+1 (541) FAR-WEST

www.ingramcontent.com/pod-product-compliance
Lightning Source LLC
Chambersburg PA
CBHW031545310726

48971CB00008B/2638